The Spa

The Spa

Michael Fowlkes

Strategic Book Publishing and Rights Co.

Strategic Book Publishing & Rights Co., LLC
USA | Singapore
www.sbpra.net

For information about special discounts for bulk purchases, please contact Strategic Book Publishing and Rights Co., Special Sales at bookorder@sbpra.net.

ISBN: 978-1-68235-400-1

Chapter 1

Beneath the stylish clothes, the flowing hair, and the beautiful lean body beat the heart of a tiger. And on rare special occasions, she'd let the tiger out of its cage.

Today was one of those days.

Jewels Martin had received the encrypted text three days earlier, and as usual, she laughed at the way she'd learned to use terminology from the spy novels she'd always loved reading. Following protocol, as she'd been taught, she responded to her *handler*, getting details on her *assignment*.

Her appointment at The Spa was for ten a.m., and she was scheduled for a full treatment, which meant she'd be off grid for hours and completely covered if anyone tried to reach her. She'd be without her phone the entire time; digital devices of any kind were forbidden while on assignment. Everyone knew the rules and obeyed them without exception.

Over the years, The Spa had carefully cultivated its elite reputation by guaranteeing absolute privacy for its clients. Along with providing first-class spa services, it also offered the perfect cover for the high-end individuals who patronized this exclusive, lavish facility.

The Spa is part of an upscale, open-air shopping complex known as Fashion Island and is one of the center's most prestigious and most popular tenants. Home to some of the most exclusive stores, restaurants, and boutiques in the world,

Fashion Island is the quintessential shopping destination of the rich and aimless, as well as an iconic Southern California tourist attraction. The wealthy patrons spend freely, not bothering to look at prices as they swipe their black-, platinum-, and gold-encrypted credit cards.

Located on a gentle slopping hillside overlooking the affluent suburb of Corona del Mar and the turquoise waters of Newport Harbor, the breathtaking views from Fashion Island span across palm-lined Pacific Coast Highway, over the harbor, and into the Pacific. On a clear day, Catalina Island can be seen twenty-six miles away. Window and patio tables at the fine restaurants are prime real estate, and while sipping a cocktail and watching the beautiful people stroll by with the scent of the sea in the air, one is easily seduced into believing that life is good ... very good.

A stone's throw away from all this glamour and extravagance is the headquarters of the Newport Beach Police Department.

***

Jewels arrived early, and was warmly greeted by one of the several young, attractive hostesses working The Spa's reception desk. An absolutely stunning woman, Jewels was just over five seven and a fit one hundred twenty-six pounds, she was blessed with flowing natural blond hair and classic deep-green eyes.

But walking up, looking at the younger versions of herself behind the counter, their innocent crystal-clear bright eyes and lean bodies made her feel old, even though they all practically bowed to her as she signed in and placed her left hand, palm down, on the desktop reader. *Shit*, she thought to herself waiting the few seconds to be automatically cleared full access, *my days are numbered here.* No matter how regimented she was with her workouts—no matter how carefully she managed her health-oriented lifestyle—the harsh truth was, she was getting older. As hard as she tried, and as successful as she was keeping herself in beautiful shape, the reality that *experience is one thing, but youth, oh precious youth,* she thought to herself, *was another altogether, and mine is all but gone.*

After being cleared, she was escorted from the main lobby. A heavy wooden door opened as they approached, being triggered from behind the reception counter, revealing a softly lit, long hallway leading to the entrance of a finely appointed private dressing lounge that was completely separate from The Spa's main salon and changing lounges. Arriving at the inner lounge's entrance, the hostess, who was leading the way, nodded politely while opening her hand in the direction of the wall-mounted retinal scan and recessed keypad. Placing her chin on the scan's soft padded front lip, Jewels looked directly at the dim red light in the center of the unit. After the light blinked green, she stepped back and punched in her code on the keypad that had become softly illuminated, before resting her right palm this time on a second reader. Within seconds, the locks clicked quietly within the heavy doors and she entered alone.

The lounge was tastefully done in dark-grained polished koa woods. Large colorful tropical plants, subtly illuminated, were strategically placed throughout the room between seamlessly framed floor-to-ceiling mirrors and etched glass panes, creating a sense of space while serving to separate the two-dozen double-louvered doors that fanned out a short distance from the entrance of the room in a serpentine wave pattern. The lush tight-pile carpeting absorbed her every step as she made her way across the room. Soft music filled the room from unseen speakers. There were no names on any of the louvered doors, only a recessed keypad next to single letters. There was no one else in the room, which wasn't unusual. Nor was it unusual for several other men and women to be in there at the same time. Over the years, Jewels had come to prefer her morning assignments, simply because the majority of the time she'd have the entire place all to herself.

Jewels' locker was located third in from the wall on the far-left side of the room, marked by only the letter C. Again, she punched in her code. As she opened the double doors, an interior light automatically went on, softly illuminating the contents. Her arms still outstretched, hands resting on the doors, looking in, she paused before entering. Even though every locker in the room was of the identical size, every locker's contents were unique.

Both sides of Jewels' were lined with clothes. Each garment professionally and perfectly tailored. Shelves along the far back wall were angled slightly down showcasing over five dozen pairs of shoes. Above the shoes were several drawers filled with an assortment of fine lace undergarments, panties, bras, bathing suits, and accessories. In the corner, adjacent to her accessories, was a built-in, angled, three-sided, floor-to-ceiling mirror. Her little locker held everything from the finest of Roberto Cavil, Stella McCartney, Prada, and Analyze Davidson, to tennis dresses and a full complement of Lululemon. Her assortment of thousand-dollar Gucci heels sat lined up proudly above a row of her Pearl Izumi running shoes. She loved her secret locker, loved shopping for the things she knew would only be worn when she was on assignment. A little shiver of anticipation sent a tingle down her spine as she finally allowed herself to step into her own little personal slice of heaven.

Today's assignment was classified "outdoor casual." She selected a colorful Asians skirt, a pair of Tori Burch sandals, and a Rebecca Minkoff shoulder bag. She changed, dressed, and was ready in less than ten minutes. Checking herself once more in the mirror, she nodded to herself, pleased with the look. Letting herself out through the back door of the dressing room, it was only a short walk along a wide hallway that ended facing two sets of elevator doors. There were no other doors or windows between the dressing room and the elevator, yet it did not feel the least bit claustrophobic. Several evenly spaced, large opaque skylights and wall sconces filled the corridor with warm light. The floor was covered by the same carpet as was in the dressing room. Several ottomans lined the walls in alcoves, and a sophisticated air-flow system made for a comfortable passage. As she arrived, the right-side elevator doors automatically opened, allowing her to step into the well-decorated private elevator. The surveillance cameras were undetectable. Once inside, she turned back, facing the doors, and the elevator automatically began its descent.

It took only a few seconds to reach the lower garage level. As the doors opened, she was greeted by a well-dressed driver. The midnight blue town car was backed directly in front of the elevator, its rear door open. The driver nodded politely as she got in, closing the door behind her. With the vehicles heavily tinted windows, it was dark inside the car except for the recessed floor lighting under the plush leather rear bench seat. Only after they'd pulled out of the private underground garage and into the bright sunlight did the rest of the familiar interior come into focus. As always, the built-in bar was fully stocked, and the driver had Pandora set to her favorite channel, Van Morrison Radio, currently playing an acoustic performance of "Here I Am" by UB40.

"Would you like anything, Ms. Jewels?" the driver asked politely once they were underway.

"Would love it if you'd swing through Starbucks."

"No problem," he answered immediately. "We have plenty of time."

Pulling up to the menu board, the driver asked Jewels what she'd like.

"Venti iced, nonfat latte with a single pump of mocha," she told him.

As he was about to speak into the board, she added, "Darryl, if you want anything, by all means, order something for yourself."

The driver smiled. "Thank you, ma'am. Kind of you to offer, and since you don't mind, I will," he said, adding to the order, "and one grande mocha Frappuccino."

"That'll be nine dollars and fifty-seven cents at the next window, please," came the pleasant-sounding response out of the speaker on the top of the menu's board.

Don't even have to get out of the car to get your crack these days, Jewels thought to herself.

A short time later they were pulling into the front gates of one of Newport's prestigious private bayfront clubs. The officer in the guard house simply nodded as the driver pulled up, waving him through without stopping. The driver continued into the club, but instead of heading straight towards the circular drive and the club's expansive grand main entrance, he made a hard left, then bore right, running parallel with the Pacific Coast Highway for a short distance, passing all the outer club buildings before making a ninety-degree right, now heading straight towards the water. He pulled up and stopped directly in front of a secluded private ramp leading down to the marina.

Getting out and opening her door, he smiled. "Thanks for the coffee."

Jewels nodded, winking at him as he took her hand, helping her out.

They immediately made their way down the ramp.

"Have a nice cruise," he added. "I'll be right here when you get back."

Stepping onto the boarding ladder of the large yacht docked directly in front of the ramp, she was politely greeted by the captain, who had been waiting on deck. Watching her approach, he lowered his eyes. "Good morning, ma'am." Tipping the bill of his white gold embossed white captain's cap, he added, "Welcome aboard."

"Thank you," she said softly.

"Your host is waiting for you in the salon," the captain added, nodding politely again before turning and heading up to the bridge. The entire transfer hadn't been seen by any other soul that wasn't directly involved.

A routine she'd been through dozens of times over the years, the next few moments used to scare her to death. The not knowing what was ahead made her so nervous that on several prior occasions she'd thought she might actually faint, but no longer. After all these years, she now relished the time she had making the short walk to the salon, allowing the unknown to fill her with anticipation. During her apprenticeship it was fear; now the mystery simply fueled her.

***

Her host had been patiently waiting on the suede leather couch in the salon, sipping a tall glass of fresh squeezed orange juice from a still partially frosted glass. The early morning editions of the *Wall Street Journal*, both the Los Angeles and NY *Times*, along with several other publications sat undisturbed on the low varnished custom teak coffee table in front of him. Well dressed in a pair of comfortable Zanelli slacks, an open-collar, off-white, long-sleeve oxford, and tan Olukais their eyes met as she opened the door.

Stepping inside the salon and gently closing the door behind her, he stood as she entered but did not approach her. The distance between them allowed both time for their basic instincts to fill one another's initial appraisals. She liked what she saw. He had clear eyes, a firm jaw, and was clean shaven. He was slightly greying but had a full head of neatly trimmed hair— early fifties, slight build, almost athletic looking, with a nice tan. She smiled as their eyes met.

"I'm Jewels," she said, closing the distance between them and extending her hand.

Taking it, he offered, "I'm Todd Windham. Would you like to sit down?"

"Thank you," she said, sitting down across from where he'd been seated.

"May I offer you anything? Something to drink?"

"No, thank you." Their eyes never left the other's.

Feeling no urgency to speak, they both sat back in the silence. She liked the fact he was comfortable with that. Most of the men she dealt with on assignment felt the need to start babbling on about something or another, but this one was different.

She studied the lines around his eyes, liking what she saw—a quiet confidence. She also sensed an inner strength behind his dark-brown eyes. *This could be fun.*

When she had sat down, she'd politely crossed her legs. Watching his eyes appraising her, she felt the first tinges of arousal. She closed her eyes, relaxed into the feeling, enjoying the moment.

Without saying a word, he stood up, walked around the coffee table, extending his hand to her. She took it, reestablishing eye contact as he approached. The electrical charge as their fingers touched sent another little wave of anticipation down her spine, making her stand as she took his hand. He turned, leading her down the interior staircase into the spacious master stateroom below. The yacht had slowly backed out of its slip and had started making its way through the harbor.

Once inside the understated, stylishly decorated stateroom, he closed the door behind them with his free hand. They stopped at the foot of the king-size bed. A beautiful tropical patterned bar cloth covered the pillow-top mattress, a free-flowing pattern of rich yellow and orange flowers blending with dark green leaves and ferns. She loved the look of that bedspread. In fact, she loved the entire stateroom. It made her feel as if she was in a tropical paradise.

This was one of the moments she loved most, waiting to see what they would do next. She'd thought she'd seen it all, but instead of this handsome stranger asking her to get undressed, or just unzipping his trousers, he gently guided her hand away from his body around the front of hers, which left her standing in front of him, facing away. Letting go of her hand, he stood silently behind her. She remained perfectly still, waiting, intrigued, wondering what he was going to do next.

He was in no hurry to unwrap her mysteries. She was a natural beauty; he'd seen that the moment he'd laid eyes on her. Now standing directly behind her, inches from her flowing blond hair, rich in texture, healthy and natural, he drank her in with slow, deep breaths. His eyes followed the outline of her body, liking everything he saw. Taking another breath, he closed his eyes, inhaling her sweet aurora—her freshly shampooed hair and subtle perfume. Taking yet another slow, deep breath, he allowed the richly aromatic fragrance to fill his senses. *Such a wonderful blend,* he thought to himself. *Citrus based, but with a hint of . . .* It took him another breath, but he identified it. *Vanilla.*

"Very nice," he said softly. "The Twenty-Four compliments you."

She was impressed. *Most men don't even know what shoes a woman is wearing or whose purse she's carrying, but this guy nails my Faubourg perfume as casually as if we'd been discussing the weather.*

A slight shiver shot up her spine as she felt both of his hands reach up from behind, under her skirt, running up the full length of her legs, his firm hands pausing on the top of her panties. He lingered there for a moment, allowing his fingers to slip in and out of the thin line of top fabric before he gently began pulling them down in one effortless motion. His hands now back on her hips, his thumbs gently applied pressure to the small of her back, coaxing her upper body to bend forward as he half guided, half lifted her until she was kneeling, face down on the edge of the bed. He gently lifted her dress, pulling the fabric up and over her now bare ass onto her back. Her womanhood was totally exposed, completely vulnerable. She took tremendous pride in not having a single hair between her legs. Velvet smooth—she glistened where she knew it counted most—knowing exactly the effect it had on men. He was no exception. She was beautiful, her womanhood inviting. Gazing at her in this position, he had become fully aroused.

"Please keep your eyes closed," he whispered.

She nodded, eyes already closed, her other senses intensifying by the second as this mysterious man continued to fascinate her. The next sound she heard was water running from the head. She heard him approach the bed again—felt him kneel between her legs—but there was no way she could have anticipated what was going to happen next.

No one had ever done anything like this to her before. The initial sensation was so foreign, so unexpected, it took her a second to even begin to comprehend what was happening— what he was doing—but as her mind wrapped itself around what was happening—the sensations pleasing, so purely sensuous— she felt herself starting to surrender to him.

10

She'd initially only felt his warm breath on the bare skin of her lower back before the warm moisture encompassed her entire womanhood.

With both hands, he'd brought it up from between her knees and was now holding it between her inner thighs. Pressing firmly for a moment, he then released the pressure, allowing time for every nerve to feel and absorb the warm moisture. He slowly began spreading the softest material she'd ever felt, opening it, unrolling it outwards across her bottom, pressing, then releasing pressure, until he'd totally wrapped her thighs, her bottom, and her entire vaginal area. She was now completely cocooned—gently wrapped, secure in an incredible sense of warmth—in a material so soft, so fine, it felt as if it wasn't even touching her skin.

His hands overlapping, working together, he continued applying steady, even pressure, before releasing, moving an inch or two, pressing, holding pressure and releasing again. His hands moved effortlessly over one cheek, around her hip, then back inside her thigh, moving up and over her vaginal area again before circling around her other side in what became one continuous flow, her body melting deeper and deeper into the moment.

There was no rush—no urgency—only a gentle, firm, nurturing, pressure. She had no idea how long he continued with what she began thinking of as some sort of cleansing ritual, but she didn't care. She was immersed in surrender, allowing her mind to slip in and out of bliss. He slowly began unwrapping the fine cloth, once again completely revealing her nakedness. She no longer felt exposed, naked, or vulnerable. Instead, she felt renewed, like a newborn baby. *Like a virgin*, she thought to herself.

The simple purity of the moment sent another wave of chills up her spine. She felt so pure—so empowered—that suddenly she wanted to make love with this man, to give herself to him.

11

What she anticipated was going to be just another assignment had transformed itself into something different, something intimate. This never happened. She felt her heart starting to race, her womanhood swelling, wanting him. It was all she could do to keep herself from flipping over and pulling him into her. But she forced herself to remain still, only to be richly rewarded, because he wasn't nearly finished.

Setting the cloth aside, he picked up a canister of sea salt he'd brought out from the head with him earlier. Pouring the salt into his hand until the crystals overflowed, he allowed them to sprinkle onto her lower back and bottom. When the crystals first began landing on her, she didn't know what it was, like gentle raindrops hitting her skin. Ever so slowly and ever so gently, he began rubbing the salt all over her bare ass and around her hips. The extreme contrast from the warm, moist velvet cloth, to the exfoliating sensations of the fine crystals against her skin were transcending, freeing any conscious thoughts, then pulling her back into her body as his hands touched a new area of skin. No sooner than she'd become aware of his hands moving over her, then off again, did she find her thoughts floating away under his touch. He slowly massaged the salt around until the pure white cheeks of her ass turned pink. He felt her inner thighs quiver as his salt-covered fingers gently caressed the outside of her fully swollen vaginal lips; she'd never felt sensations like this before in her life.

Warm water being slowly poured over the dimples in her lower back, flowing down between the heart shaped flesh of her ass, over her vagina and down the inside of her legs brought her back into her body. The warm liquid was such a sweet contrast to the salt treatment. He tenderly brushed the last traces of salt from her skin with more warm water. She'd completely surrendered herself to the pure bliss of the moment. He gently patted her dry with a soft towel before lifting her from her kneeling position, laying her down on the bed. She felt as light as a feather in his arms, her entire body floating on air.

His hands slid under the inside of her thighs, his fingers again just barely grazing her pulsating womanhood. Cradling her hips, he lifted her to his lips. Her vagina flowing with moisture, swollen, pulsating with every heartbeat, but when his tongue gently caressed to the rim of her ass—instead of where she anticipated feeling him—her entire body quivered, involuntarily contracting as his inquiring tongue began probing.

She heard herself moaning softly, the sensations becoming all-consuming.

As his tongue continued working its magic, she felt an orgasm building inside her. Her body had taken over and was about to explode. With incredible instincts, perfectly in tune with her, he sensed what was about to happen, and just as she was about to climax, he slipped effortlessly inside her, sending her into the abyss. She exploded with pleasure, her entire body quivering as wave after wave of pleasure consumed her very being.

***

Lightheaded, almost faint, she couldn't remember ever having a multiple orgasm before. Her entire body trembled as she greedily inhaled, desperately grasping to catch her breath. She became aware of the fact that he hadn't moved an inch. He'd simply wrapped his arms around her and held her tightly against his body, his manhood buried deep inside her the entire time. As she felt him starting to slowly move inside her, she realized this wasn't over.

"Easy," she heard him whisper from some distant hemisphere far, far away, "You're alright . . . you're alright. Just breathe."

The kindness and concern in his voice, reassuring her, made her head involuntary nod. "I know," somehow escaping from her lips. Still trying to catch her breath, she heard herself whispering softly. "I know . . . I'm okay."

Time stood still as fresh oxygen filled her lungs. She was soaked in perspiration. She became aware of his steady heartbeat, her head lying on his chest felt comforting, assuring, strong, and steady.

"Are you sure?" he whispered, gently brushing some locks of hair away from her face.

Her entire body glowing from within, radiating from pure, unbridled pleasure, she managed to nod. She tried to speak again, but whatever words she intended to form lost context in her bliss. Her body instinctively answered him instead with several firm vaginal contractions wrapping themselves around his hardness. He immediately responded and started moving again. She let herself go one last time, climaxing in perfect harmony as he exploded inside her. His screams of ecstasy echoing in her ears was the last thing she remembered before passing out as they melted together into an ethereal bliss.

***

She didn't realize he'd gotten up until she felt him sitting back down on the bed beside her. Her lips instantly, involuntary formed a smile.

"Here you go," he said, offering her a sip of cool water.

Eying the glass as he reached behind her neck, helping to raise her head up enough to be able to take a little sip, she managed a nod. "Thank you."

Smiling back at her, he said, "Thank you. You were incredible."

"Aren't I the one who's supposed to be telling you that?" she managed to get out sarcastically.

He smiled. "You're an incredible woman."

Their eyes met, but she broke contact, glancing away as she lowered her head back down into the pillow. He reached over, gently moving a strand of hair from across her eyes. She couldn't remember ever feeling this way on assignment. In fact, she couldn't ever remember feeling like this before in her entire life. *This isn't supposed to happen*, she thought to herself.

The consummate professional, she wasn't ready for this.

"How long have I . . . ah . . . been asleep?" she whispered, eyes closed.

"A couple hours," he answered calmly.

"What?" Her eyes snapping open. "What time is it?"

"A little after three."

"I've gotta go," she said, bolting up, almost causing herself to pass out again.

"I know," he said calmly. "That's why I woke you. Darryl is standing by."

Stunned, she blurted out defensively, wildly swinging her legs off the bed, frantically looking around for her clothes, "How do you know my driver's name?"

"When we docked," he explained, "I saw him get out of the car. So, I went up and introduced myself, told him you'd be out shortly," he continued with a hint of a smile, watching her frantically looking for her stuff.

"What else?" she snapped at him, pausing her search, realizing how schoolgirl foolish she looked holding one shoe and her panties askew in her arms.

"Nothing," he said, now fully smiling, holding out his arms innocently.

"Okay, okay," she admitted, letting out a deep breath. "I know I look stupid."

"Not at all," he assured her. "You're radiantly cute."

"Cute?" she questioned. "No one's called me that in years."

"Sorry. It's the truth. Because, Ms. Jewels, you are not only as cute as a button right now, but radiantly beautiful."

That made her smile. Taking another deep breath, glancing around the room for her other shoe, she said, "I really have to get going."

"I'll wait topside while you get dressed and walk you to your ride."

"That's not necessary," she offered lamely.

"I know," he said softly, pausing, then nodding towards the mirror in the head. "You might want to give your hair a once through." She stopped short at seeing her reflection in the mirror. Her hair was an absolute mess. Pulling a small brush out of her bag, she gingerly began working on the tangled strands. *Damn*, she thought to herself, *I am getting too old for this.*

He came up behind her, gently taking the brush out of her hand. "Sit," he instructed her. He started at the bottom of her tangled strands, working his way up, gently brushing her hair.

Her thoughts drifted back in time to when she was a child. Not since she was a little girl had anyone brushed her hair. Feelings of contentment replaced her earlier panic as she once again found herself surrendering to his touch. Between being present, feeling every brush stroke, to finding herself drifting in memories, she thought about how proud she'd been, celebrating her eighteenth birthday with her very first assignment. *So young . . . so innocent. Almost twenty years ago. No regrets.* The brush freed another few tangled strands. Her eyes still closed, she thought, *Maybe it really is time to start seriously thinking about getting out.*

It took a while, but it didn't matter any longer; time had ceased to exist. Todd managed to get through the tangled mess, and after a couple dozen full-length, deep-flowing strokes, he handed her back the brush, stood up, gently kissed the top of her head and left, allowing her time to get herself organized and dressed.

***

Todd was patiently waiting in the salon as she came up the stairs, nodding his approval. "You look beautiful."

"Not cute?" she teased him.

He smiled at her, "You will always be cute." He paused. "As well as one of the most beautiful women I've ever had the pleasure of meeting."

His forthright, open honesty made her eyes smile from within. Pausing directly in front of him, she looked up, meeting his eyes. They calmly held one another's gaze.

Not finding answers to questions she wasn't even sure she was asking, she thought about snapping off a smart-ass remark, but instead simply asked, "Will I see you again?"

"I leave this afternoon for DC."

"Oh," was all she said, trying to hide her disappointment.

"But it'll only be for a few days," he offered, extending his hand as they stepped off the yacht. "Perhaps when I return?"

Darryl opened the door to the town car as they approached.

"You know how to find me," she said, slipping into the back seat.

The men nodded at one another as Todd turned and walked away.

Her mind was spinning on the drive back to The Spa.

As they were driving over the bay bridge, Darryl inquired, "Are you alright, Ms. Jewels?" already knowing the answer because his vehicle was live fed a real-time, digital stream from the highly sophisticated wireless surveillance system The Spa utilized in all of its venues. They'd been installed to not only protect its assets, but as added insurance, just in case any video footage was ever needed to help give someone's attitude a persuasive little nudge in the right direction.

"Fine, Darryl," she answered without looking up. "I'm fine." She paused. "Thanks for keeping an eye on me."

"Ms. Jewels, you know I've always got your back."

"I know you do," she assured him, thinking to herself, *But what about my heart?*

Chapter 2

"Fucking Feds," mumbled Steel, tossing his cell into the mess of papers scattered all over his desk.

"What was that all about?" one of his men asked from behind his desk a few feet away.

"Chief says Feds want the scoop on our escorts."

"That's bullshit."

"Said he just got off the line with some DC bureau chief, and they're sending over a couple of agents tomorrow morning and want to be brought up to speed on everything we've got."

"You've got to be kidding me. We've got six months in on this, and they want to just waltz in here and take over our case?"

Steel gave his detective a glance before admitting what everyone in the Special Investigations Unit knew. "What case?"

"Okay," the detective admitted, "we don't have much."

"But a bunch of hours," interrupted Steel, "watching some pretty young ladies strolling around with a bunch of fat ol' fucks they wouldn't look twice at if there wasn't money changing hands."

"You're right, boss, but still, it's our case."

"As empty as it is."

"If we had more time, I know we could slam it shut," Steel mumbled more to himself than his detective.

"I know. But why do the Feds give a crap who's fucking who in our fine city anyway?"

"No idea," Steel answered honestly, shaking his head. "But the chief said we have to give 'em everything we've got."

"Makes me want to puke," the detective added. "Those arrogant pukes. Think they can stroll in here all high and mighty and pimp everything we've got."

"I need some air," Steel said, grabbing a faded dark-blue Patriots hoodie from the back of his chair. "Let's get out of here."

***

Five minutes later, both officers were sitting across from one another in one of the half dozen booths lining the wall of the Galley café, a small, secluded dive tucked well away from the crowds where Harbor Island Drive dead ends into the Basin Marine shipyard. A Newport fixture since 1957, the family-owned Galley is as old school as it got. An inviting little spot that has been feeding locals and Newport's men in blue the same classic diner fare since the day it opened, to this day, nothing has changed. The original, completely worn-out, deeply cracked and faded red vinyl seat covers feel like home the minute your ass slides into one.

"Afternoon, Officers," the waitress said, just to piss them off. Being undercover, she knew they hated being called out, but she did it every time they came in.

"Think one of these fine days you'll wake up and not be such a bee'atch?" Steel countered.

"Doubt it," the waitress said with a grin pinched across her thin lips, looking him in the eyes.

"Yeah, me too," Steel agreed, smiling at her, shaking his head, "too much to wish for in one life."

"The regular?" she asked, turning away, not waiting for their response, already knowing what they each wanted.

Watching her behind the counter fill an opaque muffin-topped-shaped glass that had long ago lost all its transparency with shaved ice and soda water before pumping several squirts of dark colored syrup into the glass, stirring it with a long slender spoon before adding a heaping scoop of rich vanilla ice cream, was one of the few moments in Steel's life when the world didn't seem to be filled with hate. He didn't even like root beer floats that much, but watching her make sodas or blending the occasional malt in of the dented stainless-steel canisters, the old-fashioned way, somehow soothed his scorched soul . . . if only for a few brief moments.

"How do the Feds even know we're in the middle of this case?" the detective asked, interrupting his boss's moment of bliss.

Steel had been with the Newport Beach PD ever since graduating the academy, working his way up through the ranks, he'd eventually settled into his current position, head of the Special Investigations Unit, which in Newport handled both narcotics and vice. With his years on the streets and razor-sharp instincts, Steel had developed into one of the best officers on the force. A virtual pit bull when he got on a scent, not only his unit, but the entire department held him in the highest respect.

"I'm pretty sure they're fishing."

"For what?"

"Don't have a clue," Steel admitted. "But something's got their attention."

"Way outside their normal ops."

"That's what caught my attention," Steel continued. "You nailed it back at the house when you asked why DC gives a rats ass who's paying to fuck who here in our little slice of paradise."

"They're going to be here tomorrow?"

"First thing in the morning."

"How do you want to handle it?"

21

"We'll toss some shit on the table, see if anything piques their interest and go from there," Steel said, pausing briefly before continuing. "Gut tells me they're looking for some connection, a link to another case they're working."

"That makes more sense than them being interested in some escort service."

***

First thing the next morning, a nondescript silver-grey sedan pulled into the parking lot at 870 Santa Barbara Drive, headquarters of the Newport Beach Police Department. Behind the wheel was an attractive woman in her early thirties. As she stepped from the vehicle, her lean, fit body filled out her Tehari suit perfectly, leaving little to the imagination. Exiting the passenger side was rookie agent Walter Reed.

***

"I'm Sergeant Dan Steel," Steel said, extending his hand.

"Special Agent Spring Fields."

Are you kidding me? Steel thought to himself. *Did your parents hate you?*

As the agents were shown into the SI unit, he continued introducing his team, starting with Detective Lisa Laughlin, a striking woman in her mid-twenties. Detective Laughlin looked so young she was asked to show her ID whenever she ordered a drink. With her rich tan, sun-bleached hair, athletic body, and perfect small breasts, she could easily pass for a teenager. The only real problem she ever ran into when going undercover as a high school student was keeping the boys from drooling all over her.

Detective Casey Hale, on the other hand, her male counterpart, made no effort at keeping the coeds away whenever he went undercover. "Part of the job," he'd say, shaking his head, proclaiming innocence. "Gotta blend, or those kids know something's up." The chief didn't want to even think about it.

After introductions, the group moved into a small windowless conference room where they settled in around an oval table.

"So, the chief says you're interested in meeting some of our girls," Steel asked, smirking, starting off the conversion.

"Doesn't have to be like this," Agent Fields rebutted immediately.

"The hell it doesn't," Steel shot back at her, "with the bureau's history of waltzing into local enforcement thinking your shit doesn't stink."

"Fuck you," Agent Fields snapped back at him.

"I can see everyone's getting along just fine," the chief of police said sarcastically as he came through the door unannounced, followed by his executive officer. The room went instantly silent. He let his commanding presence settle on everyone, pausing before continuing. "Good," he said, nodding while lowering himself into one of the vacant chairs at the table. "Detective Steel, would you please be so kind as to bring our guests up to speed."

Steel glared down at copies of the case folders in front of him, not looking up to meet his chief's or anyone else's eyes. "Certainly, Chief," he said respectfully, handing copies of the files across the table to the Feds. "As you are well aware of, Chief, we've had escort services targeting the citizens of our fine city here for decades. Other than a couple of low-life street operations we busted back in the day, they're now all web-based ops. So, there's been little we can do there."

"And?" the chief asked, having been fully briefed on the details of the unit's ongoing investigation.

Steel paused before continuing, "We've been working a case, and, Chief, I have to remind you, we've been assigning very few hours to this."

"I'm fully aware of assignments," the chief said.

"Yes, sir," Steel continued. "We think there might be a well-organized group working the bayfront."

"Details, please," the chief commanded.

"Sir, we have very few," Steel said, opening the case file for the first time. "A little over six months ago, April fifteen to be precise, at fourteen hundred hours, Detectives Laughlin and Hale here," he said, nodding at his detectives, "while working undercover dope on the waterfront, observed two older-looking foreign gentlemen being escorted onto a yacht by several much younger, extremely attractive ladies."

Agent Field interrupted, "Foreign-looking from where?"

Both the detectives and Steel looked to their chief for direction. He nodded, knowing their concerns in front of the Fed agents was of racial profiling. "Look," the chief said, "nothing is on the record here. Just two law enforcement agencies sharing intel, right?" he asked looking into Agent Fields' dark-blue eyes. Her slight nod gave him the answer he needed. "I think we can speak candidly."

Both the federal agents then nodded noticeably in agreement.

"They looked Iranian or Paki. I don't know; I can't tell 'em apart," Detective Hale said.

"Any photos?" Agent Reed asked.

"We weren't there for that," Hale answered defensively.

"I know; just asking was all."

"No. We don't have any images."

Steel picked up his brief. "The contrast in ages, the ratios of two to one, and the way the young ladies were dressed caught their attention. They were not able to follow up on this particular group because the primary case they were working was unfolding, but on several later occasions, the detectives revisited the same restaurant and observed similar activity. After their report, I authorized time."

"And what have you got?" the chief asked.

Steel would have loved to have snapped off some smart-ass remark, like nothing but a bad case of herpes, but knew the chief would have had his ass. "Nothing much else, sir."

"Steel," the chief said, staring at one of his top commanders.

"Honestly, Chief," Steel said. "Other than observing similar groupings at other restaurants, we don't have squat. I haven't even mounted a task force on this thing."

"Why not?" challenged Agent Fields, receiving glares from everyone except her partner at the table, including the chief. "I'm sorry," she said, immediately realizing she was out of line.

"And why not?" the chief now asked Steel politely.

"Because, sir, as you again so well know, in the past twenty-four months, we have had almost a hundred opioid-related deaths—and that's only counting kids twenty-five and younger. Kids are dying because of this shit. So, with all due respect to our guests here," Steel said, nodding towards the federal agents, "we've focused our limited resources on tracking down the scumbags that are bringing the shit in and how they're getting it into our schools, instead of chasing entitled assholes paying to get their dicks sucked."

"Black tar?" asked Agent Fields.

"Yeah, that and a shitload of oxy," Steel confirmed. Surprising himself, he was actually warming up to her. She was professional, hadn't backed down to his snide remarks, and was asking solid questions. *Maybe this won't be so bad after all*, he thought to himself.

"We talked to DEA, and they're saying the majority of the shit you're dealing with is coming up from Jalisco," Agent Fields added.

"It's from Guadalajara for sure," Steel agreed, actually engaging in a conversation with them now. "It's a much darker and gooier blend than Columbian."

"Lazy-ass Mexicans don't want to waste as much time processing their shit as their esteemed Columbian brethren to the south do."

"It's nasty shit for sure."

"Are those numbers just for Newport?" asked Agent Fields.

"Fortunately, no," the chief told her. "Covers Huntington down to Dana Point, inland up through San Juan, Rancho Santa Margarita, Mission Viejo, Irvine, and Lake Forest."

"Assuming that covers Costa Mesa as well. What about Santa Ana?" Agent Fields asked, surprising everyone with her local knowledge on how distinctively different the neighboring cities really were.

"Numbers cover Costa Mesa, but not Santa Ana. That city is a different animal altogether," the chief added.

Fields nodded in agreement. "Anyway," she said, "we understand and realize you've got your hands full. We're not here to horn in on anything you've got working. We're just trying to put some pieces together."

I knew it, Steel thought to himself. *A fishing expedition. But why? Why here? Why now? These guys wouldn't be wasting their time unless they were onto something big. Maybe it's time to play nice.*

"I wish we had more for you," Steel said, offering an olive branch. "We'd be glad to take you down to a couple of the spots we've observed the girls working. Maybe get lucky. Seeing the operation for yourselves, something'll click."

"We'd appreciate it," Agent Fields said, flashing a warm smile for the first time since they'd walked in.

"No problem," Steel added. "Glad to do it."

This little exchange made the chief smile. "Okay then," he said, getting up. "Looks like you kids are going to play nice." Addressing his lieutenant, he added, "Our work here is done." He glanced over at Steel before leaving the room, "Keep me informed."

"Always," Steel assured his commander as the chief exited the room.

Directing his attention back to the Feds, he asked, "You guys don't happen to have a change of clothes in the car by any chance?"

The agents looked briefly at one another. "That obvious, huh?"

"Yeah," Steel said. "We stroll in looking like that, and the gigs up before we even sit down."

"Understood."

Detective Laughlin jumped in, offering, "Jack's is having a sale. I was there last night, and they have some cool stuff half off. Why don't I run us over there, and we'll get you guys into something a little more casual?"

"That'll work," the agents agreed. "Thank you."

"No problem."

"After they get changed, let's meet at Billy's," Steel said, glancing at his watch, "It's a little after ten now; let's meet back up there at eleven-thirty. That should give you plenty of time."

***

A little over an hour later, Laughlin and the two federal agents walked into Billy's. Steel and Hale hardly recognized them. Laughlin had done a great job getting them outfitted—both federal agents now looked like locals. Steel and Hale stood as the three approached their table, casually shaking hands and pulling out chairs for Laughlin and Fields.

"Thank you," Agent Fields said, sitting down.

"A lady could get used to this," Laughlin added, teasing her boss.

"Don't," was all Steel told her dryly.

The group ordered drinks and waited.

***

Working plainclothes is one thing; going undercover is another world altogether. The pressure an undercover officer faces is brutal. Deep undercover is the most stressful job in law enforcement. The amount of planning, risk, and expenditures that go into an operation can pressure an officer into trying to succeed at all costs. Living a double life means isolation from family, friends, and loved ones, being removed from any direct supervision, and more often than not, not having a clue as to where the investigation stood, when it might end, or when it might all blow up. No fixed workplace or regular hours, no rules, blending as one with scumbags, corruption, drugs, and alcohol can push an individual over the line.

But none of that was on the minds of any of the veteran officers and agents sitting around the table at Billy's. They had been there for half an hour, their light conversation coming to an abrupt end when a small group of attractive young ladies began gathering at the far end of the bar about twenty-five feet away from their table, just out of earshot.

"Fuck," Steel let out, summing up everyone's immediate thoughts, "we should have sat at a closer table."

Seeing beautiful women in Newport was an everyday occurrence, but an aloof pretense about this little group's presence felt unnatural.

"What do you think?" Steel asked his detectives.

"Don't recognize any of those particular girls," Laughlin said.

"The second one in from the left, Lisa," Hale said. "I think we've seen her in here before."

"You know, I think you're right," Detective Laughlin agreed. "Wasn't she a blond?"

"Yeah, but I'm pretty sure it's the same girl."

"You're right," Lisa agreed. "She's a regular."

The officers and agents continued watching as the group grew to a dozen attractive young women. All looked to be in their early twenties, and they were all were dressed in what would have to be described as casual chic, with low-cut blouses showing off an array of digitally enhanced remastered breasts, tight shorts or short skirts revealing firm curves and slender, youthful legs. These ladies weren't Lululemon or meeting up for a shopping spree.

A short while later, an attractive woman in her early forties walked into the restaurant accompanied by a well-built younger gentleman. The couple was sharply dressed. The woman had on a smart, dark-grey, one-button jacket with a ruffled collared mock-neck tunic and a single-strand, bone-white pearl necklace. The gentleman was wearing a dark-blue sports coat over a white oxford shirt without a tie. Both had on expensive shoes. They paused just past the hostesses' station, casually surveying the room. By this time, the place had started to fill. Billy's was known for serving some of the best fish tacos in town. They used only fresh, pure-white wahoo seared in a light panko crust that simply couldn't be beat. Add a squeeze of fresh lime and a splash of white sauce, and the tender white meat simply melted in your mouth. The officers and agents had ordered the tacos and were fully engrossed with their food when the couple arrived. To the casual observer, Steel's group looked just like any other table of friends enjoying a good meal together—but not to the lady in grey.

As the hostess led the couple to their table, the lady in grey made brief eye contact with one of the girls in the group, and that's all it had taken. The lady and blue blazer were shown to a window table away from the bar. He politely pulled out the chair for her when they arrived. Once seated, with her back to the bar, he sat opposite where he had clean eye lines on both the bar and the front entrance. Steel and his entourage were positioned directly in the middle, between the newly seated couple and the girls at the bar. Within minutes after Grey's arrival, the girls at the bar began dispersing at a leisurely pace one or two at a time. Within fifteen minutes, they were all gone.

"That was weird," Agent Reed said.

"I thought for sure we were onto something there," Hale commented.

"Me too," Laughlin agreed.

"I think we were," Steel countered, "but they made us."

"No way," Hale said, defensively shaking his head.

"I think so," Steel stayed the course.

"How so?" asked Laughlin.

"That couple seated by the window over there," Steel said, barely directing a nod toward the dark-grey suit and blue blazer.

"What about them?"

"They're not together," Steel stated. "He's her bodyguard."

"How do you know?"

"Don't for sure, but he's packing, and they haven't made eye contact with one another since they came in—at least not that I've seen."

Everyone at the table waited for Steel to continue.

"There's not another person in the place that's wearing any type of sport coat or jacket. It's seventy-five degrees outside, and they walked in just before noon. So, you know he's got to be roasting in that jacket, but he didn't even think about taking it off, not even when he sat down. The bulge on his left side is hard to miss."

"What do they have to do with the girls?" Laughlin asked.

"Can't say for sure, but wouldn't everyone agree that those girls looked like they were waiting for something or someone?"

Everyone at the table nodded in agreement.

"It appears that whomever they were waiting for never showed up, so they split."

Everyone nodded again.

"But within fifteen minutes after the grey suit and blazer arrived, the girls were gone—no lunch, no hors d'oeuvres, no bill for the drinks that I could see. Nothing. Not even a trace. Like they were never even here."

"So, you think they were waiting for grey suit?" Fields summated.

"I do," Steel said, nodding. "I think we may be looking at our madam and her bodyguard."

It was all the team could do to not immediately look over in unison at the couple seated by the window, but they were all professionals and knew better. As they continued their meal, each was able to take a causal glance in the couples' direction.

"I think they had a little get-together planned. Grey suit made us and pulled the plug."

"If that's true," Hale said, "then she's good. Real good."

"What do you think tipped her off?"

"I have no idea," Steel said, slowly shaking his head. "Did anyone see her communicate with any of the girls?"

"No."

"Maybe through the waiter?"

"I don't think so. The girls started leaving almost before they were seated. I'm thinking it's straight protocol—a signal, a predetermined set of circumstances—and everyone knows exactly what they're supposed to do."

"That means they're well organized," added Fields.

"And well coached," said Reed.

"What do you say we get together for a little group photo?"

"Roger, skipper."

Everyone circled around the table, putting grey suit and blazer perfectly in the background.

"One more," Detective Hale said, zooming all the way in with his i-12 for a close-up of the couple. "Got it," he announced proudly, allowing his phone to be passed around as everyone gathered their things to leave.

"Promise to send that to me," Fields said.

"For sure," Lisa answered in her best Valley girl voice as Fields picked up the bill.

"Thanks, but I'll get that," Steel said, extending his hand.

"Not this time," Fields said, smiling. "We appreciate your time."

"That's it?" Steel said, a bit shocked.

"For now. Maybe you could zip the photos over when you have a minute."

"Will do it right now," Hale offered. "What's your email?"

Once outside, Steel closed his eyes for a moment, waiting for the valet, feeling the sunshine on his face.

"Feels good," Fields stated flatly.

Steel nodded. It was indeed another beautiful day along the coast in Southern California.

"It's easy to see why people love living here so much," Fields added.

Their eyes met for a brief, probing moment.

Steel asked, "You're LA field office, right?"

Fields nodded with a look that said it all, adding with a slight smile, "What did you think? That they'd send agents from Washington?"

"Then we're practically neighbors."

"Yeah, right," Fields said sarcastically, holding out both her hands, palms up, imitating a scale weighing the two options. "Newport or LA? Let me think . . ."

"Different worlds."

"That's for sure." Fields confirmed, pausing. "Thank you again." Their eyes met. "For being . . ."

"So cooperative," Steel said playfully, finishing her thought.

"Yeah. For being so cooperative," she said, smiling.

"Here to serve and protect," Steel said, never breaking eye contact.

As the valet pulled up in Laughlin's vehicle, Steel felt a twinge of regret creeping in, realizing he may never see Fields again. He reached out, gently touching her arm. He uttered, "If you need anything . . ."

"Thanks," Fields said, nodding as the valet opened the passenger's side front door for her.

Tipping the valet, Laughlin said over the top of the car before jumping in, "I'll drop our guests off at their car and see you guys back at the office."

Steel didn't take his eyes off the car as they pulled out of the parking lot and drove away. In his peripheral vision, Steel saw Hale eyeballing him after not having missed their little exchange of pleasantries.

"Don't say it," Steel said.

"I'm just saying, boss." Steel gave him a sideways glance, but Hale couldn't resist. "She's a damn good-looking agent."

"Not another word," Steel warned.

"Okay, okay," Hale said, surrendering with a smile. "You're the boss."

***

Inside the restaurant, the couple sitting at the window in the dark grey suit and blue blazer had been silently observing the group. Blazer had gotten up, watched their exodus, and was now reporting to the lady in grey.

"Two vehicles," he said. "The first a four- or five-year-old, midnight-blue, four-door Beemer 750. The younger of the two women was driving. The older woman got in the passenger seat, and one of the two younger men got in the back."

"Which one?"

"The one wearing the light-blue Salty Crew shirt, tan slacks, sandals, but looked like he'd never been in the sun," Blue blazer told her, watching Grey before continuing. She nodded for him to do so. "The second vehicle was a two-door, metallic-grey Lexus LX, and the older of the two remaining men got behind the wheel."

"The younger sandy-blond gentleman was the passenger?"

"Correct," answered blazer.

"Which direction did they head?"

"Both vehicles turned south."

"Thank you," the lady in the dark-grey suit said, politely nodding to herself.

Blazer waited patiently. He'd been working with her for almost a decade. Starting as her driver, his devotion and keen senses had moved him up the line until now he was not only her driver and personal bodyguard, but her confidant and friend. They'd never had sex. Even though she was an extremely attractive woman, he had no intention of ever venturing anywhere close to crossing that line. She hadn't pursued it, so neither had he. He loved his job, and pussy really didn't interest him all that much anyway.

"What was that all about?" he asked, sitting back down.

"Just a little game I play to amuse myself," she said, smiling.

He again waited patiently. A big, strong man. Six feet and an easy two hundred twenty pounds of lean mass, he moved with grace and cat-like instincts. To see him sitting there patiently, like he was with Grey, was almost comical.

"I enjoy paying attention to how people act," Grey continued. "I like watching their behavior, how they interact, body language, facial expressions," she said, having another sip of her pomegranate martini.

Blue blazer nodded.

"More than anything," she continued after a moment savoring the smooth liquid, "I look for inconsistencies—anything unnatural, that doesn't fit, or feels forced—then try and figure out why."

"It was the younger sandy-blond guy, wasn't it?" Blazer blurted out excitedly. "I've seen him in here before—him and that younger chick, the blond. I thought they were a couple," he paused, "but not today."

"Exactly," Blazer said, smiling. "Nice observation."

"I noticed them as soon as we walked in," he continued.

"So did I," Grey said, continuing their train of thought. "But," she said, pausing, "they weren't sitting together."

"Really?" Blazer asked. "That was it?"

"Initially, yes," Grey told him. "That's what caught my attention. It didn't feel right, them not seated next to one another. Couples, especially young couples, always sit together at restaurants in a group if they're not on a duce facing one another. The older man and woman were too young to be their parents, nor were they interacting like old friends. Initially, I thought maybe co-workers. As individuals, in silhouette, they were fine, but as a group . . . they just didn't blend naturally."

"What do you mean silhouettes?" Blazer asked.

"Tradecraft," Grey told him, "for personal appearances." Then announced flat out, "Ninety-percent sure they were cops."

Blazer had long ago learned never to question her instincts or second guess her, and as surprised as he was, he didn't burst out with something stupid like, "Are you sure?" Instead, he quietly asked, "Do you think they're onto us?"

She tilted her head, asking more to herself, "Why else would they be hanging around in here?"

Blazer shrugged his shoulders. He knew when to keep his mouth shut. She was a thousand times more intelligent than he was, and he knew it. He respected her more than anyone he'd ever known. He admired how incredibly intuitive she was.

After a while she added patiently, as if teaching a child, "I'm never a hundred-percent sure, but over the years I've learned to trust my instincts. It's not always easy to do, because more often than not those instincts are a royal pain in the ass, red flags and warning signals going off at the worst possible times, but I've learned to trust them. I felt something was wrong the minute I recognized that younger couple. From there, I started concentrating on that group, and the more I observed the interactions around their table, the more confident I became. The fact they posed for those lame-ass photos confirmed it, making sure to frame us in the background. I'm sure they'll have eight-by-ten glossies of us printed out by the time we leave here and pinned on some whiteboard."

Blazer nodded in agreement with everything she was explaining.

Grey smiled at him. "Further confirmation was that they left as soon as our girls were gone."

"What about their cars, or the fact they both turned south?"

"My guess is they're driving a confiscated vehicle."

"Why?"

"Because the older guy's clothes didn't match the price tag on that Lexus. He was wearing Macy's, at best, more likely crap off the rack from Kohl's or Penney's.

"And the fact they both turned left?"

"That's an easy one," Grey answered with a grin. "Either irrelevant, or they headed south towards the PD."

"Think we've got anything to worry about?"

Grey paused, "No. The girls knew what to do and handled themselves flawlessly. But we're on their radar now, that's for sure. So, from here on, everything's by the book. No exceptions."

Nodding his head in agreement, he said, "Understood."

Chapter 3

The Spa's operational control center was quantum leaps ahead of anything any branch of any government in the free world had in operation. The assets The Spa deployed were years ahead of being leaked to the chosen few as circumstances dictated. The spacious room, located on the top floor of the Fashion Island building, was connected with over a dozen virtually identical Spa operational centers across the globe. To say the business of pleasure was alive and flourishing would be a vast understatement.

If an individual were to actually glimpse the enormous inner workings and minutely detailed complexity of The Spa, it would be so overwhelming as to seem out of this world. The endless and seemingly unpredictable ebb and flow of world economics simply had no effect on The Spa, because in fact, they were the one's controlling those very ebbs and flows.

Even though the affluent walk amongst us, they live in a world far, far away from us mere mortals.

The Spa had slowly but steadily evolved over the past seventy-five years into the most efficient covert operation in the history of mankind. Operating completely below the radar, for all intents and purposes, The Spa didn't even exist—except there it was, in plain sight, with a logo and sign on the front door welcoming members and guests alike.

On the surface, each of the Spas the world over appear to be nothing more than upscale spas filled with clients looking to be pampered with a variety of custom packages and treatments, from Swedish, aromatherapy, and deep tissue massages, to salt-glow full-body exfoliations, facials, microdermabrasion, and Brazilian waxing. There were also full hair and nail salon services, workout rooms, personal instructors, lifestyle trainers, indoor lap pools, private saunas, Jacuzzis, meditation rooms, and oxygen booths. Packages were filled with services that nourished one's soul from the inside out or from the outside in—whichever one prefers—reawakening the senses, rejuvenating the body, mind, and spirit with natural supplements, lotions, and oils. Private rooms, couple's messages, and common areas were readily available to anyone with the price of admission. Once one stepped inside The Spa, it became all but impossible to not melt into its mission statement to provide each and every guest a unique, exquisite experience of total harmony in mind, body, and soul.

An absolute first-class facility, The Spa's exceptional service, it's impeccable attention to detail and incomparable hospitality exceed every expectation of even the wealthiest and most pampered of its guests. Being known as "a regular" at The Spa was as socially critical to the world's upper-class elite as was attending major political dinners, socials, or Hollywood premiers that dotted high society's calendars annually. Simply put, The Spa was the place to be and be seen.

If anyone cold called or entered the premises uttering any words other than the introductory code of the inner circle verbatim, they were instantly, seamlessly classified as one of The Spa's many welcome and pampered guests, but certainly not one of the few. Welcome guests were The Spa's cover—the reason it could flourish and fully function in plain sight without arousing a single suspicion. Welcomed guests were pampered and treated the world over to nothing but the finest of services.

But for the few, there were unlimited services offered exclusively to those granted access to The Spa's inner sanctuaries. Once obtaining VIP clearance, individuals had their palm and retina scans archived into an encrypted database and were issued their own personal access code. A combination of entering the code and matching physical scans provided these individual's full access. Of course, the additional precautions instilled by The Spa's state-of-the-art security systems were never made known to the individuals. As in most spas, there were certain phrases that opened the door to other "special services." Happy endings were nothing compared to what was available behind closed doors to the few.

What went on behind the scenes on the other side of The Spa's soundproof inner walls, available to only the few, was another world entirely. Not only did The Spa provide unlimited, extravagant services to the few, but it owned mega-yachts, luxury penthouse suites, and private estates in most affluent neighborhoods surrounding all of its worldwide locations. The Spa also owned a fleet of Citation CJ3s that were just a call away to the few.

***

The town car slipped virtually unnoticed into The Spa's private garage. Darryl pulled up into the exact spot where he'd picked Jewels up exactly five hours earlier. Opening the door, he nodded politely.

"Thank you, Darryl," Jewels said, leaving the vehicle and walking into the open elevator door.

No buttons to push this time. The elevator was on auto, stopping a floor below the dressing lounge. Initially, Jewels thought these debriefings were a bit extreme, but as the hazards of her profession became painfully clear, she now embraced the procedures. Several small rooms, all facing the elevator, fanned out, forming a sweeping circular arch away from the elevator. Each room was identical in size, fairly typical of any examination room found in most upscale doctor's offices, except these rooms were all done in soothing light-mauve tones and illuminated by soft recessed lighting. A Craftmatic adjustable bed covered in a clean, crisp, white sheet was complemented by a single deluxe Clinton Bariatric blood-drawing chair. The rooms were spotless.

Jewels entered one of the rooms, closed the door behind her, and got undressed. Pulling on the open-back gown hanging on the back of the door, she sat down in the padded chair. Within seconds, a technician knocked and entered without waiting for an answer. He was carrying a light-blue, covered plastic lab kit. He nodded politely and smiled, noticing Jewels already had her arm out and was making a fist. He sat down, wrapped a thin rubber strap around her left bicep, and took out three red-topped vials. Tapping her forearm for a suitable vein, he carefully inserted an ultra-thin needle. The first vile instantly filled.

Removing the first vile, he inserted the second, and as it filled, he said, "You no longer need to make a fist."

With the third vial filled, he placed a small cotton ball over the needle as he removed it. "Hold this, please," he instructed her, nodding toward the cotton ball. Placing all three vials back into the kit, he took out a roll of pink flexible tape and wrapped it once around her arm.

She stood and moved to the table. Laying back, she placed her feet into the stirrups.

"May I?" asked the technician again respectfully. Jewels nodded. He lifted her gown and gently swabbed her urethra. Moments later, she felt him do the same to her anus. The last swab was from the inside of her mouth. "You're all set. You can get dressed now."

"Thank you," Jewels said, sliding off the table. In less than ten hours she'd know if she'd been exposed to any STDs. Every agent went through the same debriefing procedure after every assignment. No exceptions. Knowing every agent was clean going into an assignment, if any ever came back positive, The Spa knew exactly what client or clients the agent had been engaged with, and they were forever blacklisted. Jewels only knew of one such incident in her twenty years with the company, and that was a long, long time ago. No one wanted anything to do with STDs, so every precaution was taken. Manual testing was performed on all VIPs annually as well, protecting and assuring both agents and clients that all participants were clean. No one paying the fees the few were shelling over was ever going to want to have to wear a condom or worry about going home infected to a husband or wife.

All these protocols combined to make The Spa the most elite and successful organization of its kind the world had ever known.

Ten thousand dollars wealthier, and thirty minutes after her debriefing, Jewels walked out The Spa's front doors at the exact moment Todd was lifting off from John Wayne Airport in one of The Spa's private jets toward Washington, DC.

***

"How was your day, honey?" Tyler asked casually as she walked out onto the front deck of their bayfront home where he'd been reading the paper.

A successful media strategist specializing in identifying search patterns for specific businesses, Tyler's unique ability to move his client's social platforms to the very top of the charts not only made him one of the most sought-after algorithm gurus in the business, but a wealthy man as well. Over the years, Tyler had consulted for and then turned down lucrative positions with some of the giants of technology, including Amazon, Apple, and Google, because he coveted his freedom and lifestyle. Home businesses were alive and flourishing along the shores of Newport Harbor.

"Interesting," was all she offered, sitting down next to him, kicking off her sandals.

Putting down the *Daily Pilot* he'd been reading, he looked over at her. "Really. How so?"

Slipping her arm under his and giving him a kiss on the cheek. "Nothing really." She paused. "Nice day," she commented nonchalantly, changing subjects, looking out across the calm waters of the bay surrounding the small enclave of two hundred forty-nine homes, one of which was theirs, all situated around the central turning basin of Newport Harbor.

Established in 1937 on what most folks thought at the time to be nothing more than muddy tidal swamp land, this tiny, exclusive, gated community had evolved over the years from summer beach cottages, once boarded-up and left unattended during the winter months, into a prospering intimate community featuring a unique blend of pristine private beaches, private docks, winding streets shaded by huge ficus trees and hundred foot palms, open grassy parks, and charming homes bordered by lush lawns and colorful gardens.

Jewels loved living there. She'd been born just up the road at Hoag Hospital and had been raised in Bayshores. Over the years, she'd gotten to know just about every family living there. Even though Newport is in the middle of the sprawling metropolis of Southern California, somehow this unique community was able to create, and still maintain today, a feeling of what it's like living in small town USA— a community where neighbors know, care about, and look out for one another, a place where kids can play in the streets, on the beaches, in the parks, or at a neighbor's house without causing parents any concerns or worries. Jewels believed there was no better place in the world to call home. She loved living there.

Growing up, she had exposure to expanding and challenging social, moral, and political changes that were being driven by the music and entertainment industries to the north while still having her being securely rooted and nurtured in strong family and community values. She wouldn't have traded being raised there for anything in the world.

After graduating from Newport Harbor High School, she'd opted for UCLA, but not before dealing with a major battle that still rages on today between her dad, once a standout football player at USC, and her mom, an alumnus of UCLA. Listening to them argue over the most trivial details about which institution of higher learning was better, as they have since they met following the "big game" back in the day, Jewels was amazed how they'd managed to stay married all these years. One would have thought it was the Hatfields and McCoys going at it. In truth, a large segment of the population in Newport is divided fairly equally between the two outstanding universities, but like many families throughout the southland, with alumni from both schools, somehow everyone manages to get along. How four years affect the next forty of your life was still an enigma Jewels found fascinating to ponder.

"Indeed it is," Tyler agreed, waiting patiently, watching her thinking to herself.

"What is?" Jewels asked.

"That it's a beautiful afternoon."

"Oh," was all she murmured, having gotten lost in her thoughts.

Having wisely learned over the years that she would tell him whatever was on her mind only when she was ready, he didn't probe, didn't pressure her. They'd been through so much together and had worked so hard to get where they were today, he was perfectly content to just sit together with the lady he had come to love and cherish.

"Just another day in paradise," she finally offered.

They sat for a long time. Neither feeling a need to talk. She nestled her head up under his arm.

"Everything alright?"

"Yeah," she said, pausing. "I'm thinking about quitting."

"Really?"

"Thinking about it," she nodded.

He held her, waiting patiently.

"I certainly don't need the money anymore," she stated flatly.

It had ceased being about the money years ago. They both knew that, but when she'd first started, the money had been all that it was about. She had no problem separating herself, her real life, from the job. Love was what she made with the men in her life she chose to be with. Sex is what she'd perfected to earn a living. Simple as that. When she was on assignment, it was work, period. Nothing more, nothing less. The money had always been incredible. It had put her through UCLA and later had helped pay for her dad's cancer treatments. It had made it possible for her to go in with Tyler and together make the down payment on their house. Her earnings had helped them to have the house paid off in less than five years. Her diversified global municipal funds were well established and earning as well. For all intents and purposes, she was financially set for life.

"That's for sure," he confirmed. "We're both pretty well set. I've got everything I need right here," he added, giving her a little squeeze.

"Sometimes I forget how truly lucky I am having you," she said, looking up into his eyes. He was the big brother she never had. "There aren't many men who understand or could handle what I do."

"I've been okay with your job since the day we met."

"I know."

Even though she was contractually bound to never disclose what she did for a living with anyone, other than discussing her physical therapist/personal trainer cover, it hadn't taken Tyler long to figure things out.

"You're my double-O," he said, giving her a little squeeze. "You know I don't care what other people think. Most of 'em have their heads so far up their asses anyway, who gives a crap what they think. They can't even get their own shit together. All the while, sitting back, judging, condemning others from their high atop their self-righteousness, as if God himself came down and gave them keys to the throne. Fucking politicians are the worst," he said, tapping the paper's headlines. "Goddamned hypocrites."

"Take a deep breath, honey," Jewels suggested softly.

Doing so, he agreed. It was far too beautiful of an afternoon to get wound up over the dismal state of affairs the country was in. "A waste of time worrying about shit we can't control."

"Couldn't agree with you more," Jewels whispered.

"I hate to break this little party up, but a hot bath sounds good."

"Want me to scrub your back?"

Their eyes met as Jewels countered, "What have you been trying to convince me of lately? How do you put it?" she asked, pausing. "That you are not as good as you once were, but you're better than you ever were once?"

"Now you're asking for it," he challenged her.

"Bring it on, big boy," she teased, extending her hands and wiggling her fingers teasingly towards her breasts. "I'm ready if you are."

They'd had sex once in high school, and it had been a typical teenage sexual disaster. Afterwards, they'd realized romance wasn't in the cards between them, and they'd become best of friends and over the years had grown to love one another unconditionally, without any of the inherited tension a physical relationship brings with it.

He paused, taking a deep breath, surrendering, giving her a sweet kiss on the back of her delicate hand instead of taking her up on her offer. "Maybe when we're old and grey and love is done with us, we could give it another try," he offered, knowing they both knew that day would never come.

"I'm yours for the taking, any time, any place," she said lovingly.

"If only you had different plumbing," Tyler smiled into her eyes, "my life would be complete."

Standing up, stretching like a lynx, she bent over, giving him a little kiss on his forehead before heading inside.

***

Jewels drew her bath as hot as she could stand it. She lit a couple of candles and considered adding a little rose quartz but opted instead for her favorite, vanilla. As the few drops of the pure essence hit the water, they instantly filled the room with a warm comforting aroma. Disrobing, she lowered herself into the hot water, laying her head back on a rolled-up towel.

It had only been a couple hours since her assignment with the stranger, but she couldn't get him out of her mind. She'd never felt even the most remote connection with a target in the past, but then again, no man had ever treated her like he had. *Fucker*, she thought to herself, sliding into the bath.

Time has a way of sorting things out, and she just needed a little of it right now. *Quiet time, a bedrock of stability*, she thought to herself, her emotions running out of control.

Immersed, the steaming hot water working its magic, her muscles began letting go, and the anxiety slowly started draining out of her system. Taking several deliberate, slow breaths, inhaling deeply through her nose, feeling the fresh oxygen filling her lungs, rejuvenating her, she'd hold it for a heartbeat before contracting her abdominal muscles and thoroughly exhaling through her mouth. Another deep breath, *There's nothing more to be done right now*. The sweet vanilla filling her senses softening the edge off her thoughts. Glancing at the room through half-closed eyes, she noticed the mirrors fogging in the candlelight before finally closing her eyes with one last deep breath.

Emotions and thoughts never cease, but instead of trying to put the pieces together, as she'd been doing ever since she'd gotten home, she was now allowing her mind to roam free—to go wherever it wanted, without trying to control it or make sense of things. She began slipping deeper and deeper into herself, getting out of her own way. Lying almost weightless in the warm water, she let herself be, her mind naturally, instinctively delving towards the inner comfort of her being.

She imagined herself lying on the surface of the ocean. She saw tiny bubbles rising up from the depths deep below. The bubbles grew larger and larger, expanding as they neared the surface. The worrisome seas she'd found herself in earlier, boiling around her with raw emotions, as she continued allowing her mind to roam free, she found herself, instead of being encapsulated by her thoughts, that she was now experiencing them at subtler and subtler levels, tiny bubbles instead of boiling water, slowing riding with them to the surface, surrounding them instead of the other way around.

As she floated up with each new thought, her perspective grew sharper, clearer. No longer feeling overwhelmed and out of control, instead she accepted the fact that her encounter this afternoon was really just that, an unexpected encounter while on assignment. She certainly hadn't expected it, nor had she been prepared for it, but it had happened.

The intense sensations of his touch, creating such intoxicating feelings of pleasure. Her body releasing wave after wave of endorphins, being overwhelmed with pure physical sensations, was all, she now realized, she was really dealing with. *I'm in the business of providing pleasure, not being the receiver. That's all this is.*

The fact she'd allowed herself to be completely overwhelmed on assignment was the real issue. Or so she tried telling herself. *Unto thy own self be true . . . fucking Shakespeare,* she thought, knowing the soul never lies, and with another deep breath, she found herself floating up again, surrounding a tiny bubble of fear. Watching it rise, she realized having become so self-sufficient, so self-reliant, over the years, that she was always in control and relished being in control. No one had forced her out of that comfort zone in how long, she thought to herself. A shiver shot through her spine, bringing her back to the surface, the bubble exploding around her.

Since she could remember, mentally forcing herself to take another deep breath, the question she found herself asking riding up on this bubble was, *So what are you going to do now, Miss Smarty Pants?*

A few more deep breaths. *I love my life, but maybe, just maybe* . . . was the last thing she remembered before total surrender filled her from the inside out and she found herself floating in a sea of love.

Since the beginning of time, life-changing transformation comes only when individuals surrender themselves to their souls, to their higher beings, to God—to whatever you want to call it. This is, and will forever be, the one absolute truth about mortals. Jewels continued breathing, her chest rising and falling with each new breath, with each new thought. Then, from deep within her soul, it came to her. At first, just a tiny spec of a bubble rising up from deep within her, but as she wrapped herself around the thought, embracing it as it continued expanding, filling her consciousness, it became crystal clear what she was going to do, what she had to do.

Chapter 4

Samantha lived alone in a quaint 1940's Cape Cod style oceanfront cottage in the exclusive gated community of Emerald Bay. She loved the place and relished the fact that after her divorce she'd purchased the old cottage with no intentions of tearing it down and rebuilding like all her surrounding neighbors had done. Instead, she'd supervised a complete retrofit, bringing the place back to all its original charm and simplicity. The bay itself was considered to be one of the most beautiful on the coast. Few that have ever been there would argue the point.

A gently sloping white-sand, crescent-shaped beach, majestically framed on either end by steep rocky cliffs protruding into the sea, isolated this near half-mile stretch of paradise from outsiders. This was Samantha's front yard. From her house she could watch the waters changing colors. As the waves broke, washing ashore, the white foam turning into a soft turquoise color over the shallows before returning into the incredible dark blue infinity that is the Pacific. The place was intoxicating.

Samantha had been sitting contentedly on her porch in her favorite chair, wrapped in a soft blanket, sipping a cup of hot green tea and lemon. She watched a pair of dolphins playing in the surf line as the morning's rays began filling the day. Her phone vibrated.

"What's up, girl?" she asked her best friend.

"You up for breakfast?" Jewels asked.

"Sounds good," Samantha volunteered.

"I'm on my way," she said, knowing Sam would be there.

"Nice. I'll see you in a few."

About fifteen minutes later they were walking along the water's edge, heading away from Samantha's house. There wasn't another soul on the beach. By the time Jewels had gotten there, the sun had made its way up and over the foothills behind the bay, filling the air with warming rays, ushering in another beautiful spring morning. The girls' footprints were covered, then washed away by gentle waves creeping up the beach with the incoming tide.

"So, what's up?" Sam asked.

Jewels hesitated, looking her friend in the eye, lowering her head. She'd decided last night to lay it all out on the table, starting at the beginning, leaving nothing out, but as she started to speak, nothing came out.

Sam reached over, putting an arm around her best friend, pulling their heads together, holding her tight.

Jewels was now sobbing.

Samantha just held her, letting her cry herself out.

Finally, after soaking the shoulder of Samantha's cotton blouse, Jewels was able to mutter, "I'm sorry. I'm so sorry," before another wave of gut-wrenching sobbing consumed her. She was crying like an infant in her friend's arms, unable to stop.

Samantha knew to do nothing more than just hold her friend, asking no questions, being there for her completely, silently waiting. The sobbing lasted easily another ten minutes.

"I'm so sorry, Samantha, but I've been keeping this secret from you for a long, long time. In fact, ever since we first met."

Samantha leaned over, took Jewels' head in her hands, and kissed her on the forehead. "I love you, Jewels. I love you like the sister I never had, and no matter what, nothing, and I mean nothing will change that."

Jewels' eyes filled with tears again as their eyes met again before she flat-out stated, "I'm an escort."

Samantha was so relieved, having conjured up the worst possible scenarios about Jewels being diagnosed with terminal cancer or some other horrible disease, she burst out laughing in relief. "I thought you were going to tell me you were dying or something."

"Do you understand what I just told you?"

"Yeah, of course, I heard you. It's no big deal."

"No big deal! What are you talking about? I tell you I'm an escort and you say it's no big deal?"

"I'm telling you, it's no big deal. Not to me."

Jewels were shocked. She'd been worried sick her friend would hate her. She didn't know what to say.

"But if it is to you," Sam added, "and you've been doing it all these years, then yeah, you've got a problem."

"I put myself through school as an escort."

"More power to you," Samantha said, still feeling so relieved and grateful nothing was wrong with her friend.

"An escort," Jewels said slowly, as if her friend didn't know what she meant. "An elite call girl."

"I heard you, and I know what an escort is, and once again, it's no big deal."

"But what about the fact I never told you?"

"Now we've got twenty years' worth of untold stories to get caught up on."

Jewels couldn't believe how understanding Samantha was being. Looking her in the eye, she asked, "So you're alright with what I've been doing?"

"Absolutely. In fact," she said pausing, "I think I may even be a little bit jealous."

"What?"

"You've been getting paid for what I've been doing all these years for free," Samantha added.

"You are unfucking believable," Jewels said, shaking her head. "I was so worried how you'd react. I was so afraid you'd hate me for not telling you."

"Not at all," Samantha assured her. "We all have our little secrets. Yours, maybe not so little. But still, what we do behind closed doors is no one's business but our own."

"You blow me away, Sam," Jewels added, "you really do."

"But I want details, lots and lots of juicy details."

"In time, no problem."

"Blow by blow," Sam added.

"You are a sick individual."

"I know."

They continued walking until they reached the far north end of the beach. Turning around, they were now facing the sun. Jewels closed her eyes, absorbing the warmth of the rays on her face. Eventually, she smiled, asking, "So?"

"What?" Samantha gently probed.

"So, what do you think?"

"Where do I sign up?"

"Seriously."

"I am," Sam laughed as she peeled off her coverup and headed for the water, with Jewels right behind her.

Diving into the gentle surf, they swam out together past the surf line before turning around and heading back towards shore, just long enough to get their hearts pumping and their blood flowing. They'd trotted back up through the sand, to Sam's house, rinsed off, and were drying their hair, deciding where to go for brunch.

"Let's go up to the Beachcomber," Samantha suggested. "How does that sound?"

"Perfect," Jewels answered without hesitation. "I love that place."

"Me too, but only during off-season."

"Goes without saying. Peak it's a Disney family nightmare on the beach."

A few minutes later, the girls were seated in the small café, which was located in Crystal Cove, on the sand and right next to the water.

"Every time we come there, I can't help but think how cool it is that they filmed *Beaches*, right here, right where we're sitting," Jewels said.

"Thank God for you, my friend, the wind beneath my wings," Samantha hummed, altering the lyrics to Jeff Silber's masterpiece of a song.

"I wouldn't know what I'd do without you," Jewels responded openly.

"Yes, you would," Samantha assured her with a warm smile.

"I could, but how can anyone get through this life without true friendship is beyond me."

"Not very easily, and for sure not very happily. It's really what it all comes down to."

"What's that?"

"The people we love."

Their conversation lightened as they shared the cafe's mouthwatering coconut-macadamia pancakes and an egg-white frittata with organic spinach, tomatoes, mushrooms, and provolone cheese.

Chapter 5

On the seventeenth floor of the 11000 Wilshire Boulevard building in Los Angeles, Special Agent Fields was summoned by her section chief.

"Come in," he said as Fields knocked on the frame of his open door. "Have a seat." He flipped through her summary report from her day with the Newport cops. "Anything additional?"

"No, sir," Fields told him. "Report covers it all."

"So, they really don't have anything?"

"As far as the escort scene, yes, sir, that is correct."

He continued reviewing her detailed report. "Fields, what's your gut on this?"

This surprised her. Normally the chief could give a shit about an agent's feelings. Everything relevant goes in the report. Period. Cut and dried. Facts and facts only. Everything else is nothing more than noise and has no place in the agency. "My gut, sir?" she asked.

The section chief glanced up from his notes, meeting her eyes. "Yes, Fields, your gut feelings on this." He paused. "Your report is fine," he added, assuring her nothing was wrong. "You're a damn good agent with good instincts; that's why I'm asking for your overall feelings about the case."

My feelings, she thought to herself, *are you kidding me? How about the fact I haven't been able to stop thinking about Steel since I drove out of that damn parking lot? How I'm hoping it's him every time my cell pings. Chief, are those the feelings that you're looking for? Or how about knowing about how sick and tired I am living the job. How I'm sick of being alone, going home every night to an empty apartment. Meaningless one-night stands. Want me to keep going?*

Seeing her boss looking up at her from the report snapped her out of it.

"Sir, they're dealing with a minor prostitution problem. Nothing more. Typical Craig's List type solicitations. A dying breed with Tender, Grinder, and all the new apps out there. Hookups are just a swipe away. It's all in the report."

"I know. I read it. I'm interested about anything you observed that wouldn't normally go on record."

"Chief, may I speak openly?"

"Absolutely, Fields, that's what I'm asking you to do."

"Their Special Investigations Unit is on top of what's going on. Their lead guy," she paused so she wouldn't appear obvious, "a Sergeant Steel, is sharp, street wise, knows where to look, but there's really nothing to look for. They have what appears to be some organized biz going on down there. We caught a glimpse of a stable—a madam keeping it low profile, upper-end restaurants and most likely upper-end hotels as well, but discreet, clean. There are no street solicitations, nothing that's going to make anyone look bad. Business as usual, as far as Walter and I could tell."

"Anything else?"

"Drugs," Fields answered honestly. "Those rich millennials like their dope."

"Thank you, Agent Fields."

"Do you want us to follow up with Newport PD?" Fields asked hopefully.

"Give 'em a courtesy reach-around, but unless something breaks, we're done."

"Roger, Chief," Fields said, getting up and leaving his office.

That was fucking weird, Fields thought to herself, walking back to her desk.

***

Created in 1947, the Central Intelligence Agency is an independent United States government agency responsible for providing national security intelligence to senior United States policymakers. It is manned by an elite corps of some of the finest men and women serving our nation who put "country first and Agency before self." The CIA conducts clandestine missions and collects HUNINT (actionable human intelligence) worldwide. On September 6, 2011, David Petraeus was appointed by President Obama as the director of the Central Intelligence Agency (D/CIA) and confirmed by a majority of the United States Senate.

Within the CIA, under the Department of Homeland Security (DHS), is a division known as the Secret Service. Among other duties, the Secret Service is authorized by law to protect the president, the vice president (or other officer next in the order of succession to the Office of the President should the vice presidency be vacant), the president-elect, the vice president-elect, the immediate families of the above individuals, and former presidents and their spouses for their lifetimes, except when the spouse divorces or remarries. In 1997, legislation became effective limiting Secret Service protection to former presidents and their spouses for a period of not more than ten years from the date the former president leaves office, making Bill and Hillary Clinton the last to receive lifetime protection.

Additionally, the CIA is responsible for the security and safety of visiting heads of states of foreign governments and their entourages, other distinguished foreign visitors to the United States, and official representatives of the United States performing special missions abroad as directed by the president, and other individuals as designated per executive order of the president.

The Central Intelligence Agency is accountable to, in this order, the president of the United States, Congress, and the American taxpayer.

The CIA and FBI have never played well together.

***

Moments after Fields left the office of her section chief, he was on an encrypted line into the top floor of a secure building located in the 300 block of 7th Street SW in the 703 area code of Washington, DC.

When he heard the metallic "you are connected," the section chief uttered two words, "We're clear." The connection instantly went dead.

Assholes, he thought to himself, replacing the phone. *This fucking job has gotten so twisted nothing makes sense anymore.*

***

Instead of returning to her desk, Agent Fields headed for the elevators. Her pay grade gave her automatic clearance to the heliport rooftop area on top of the Wilshire building. Stepping out of the elevator, she slid her ID card through the scanner. The thick metal, lead-lined door unlocked, but she needed to lean into the heavy door and push with both of her arms to open it. The blinding sunlight hit her directly in the face. She instantly slid down the pair of new Kaenon sunglasses she'd bought the day before when they were in Newport. She loved them because they had the clearest, sharpest polarized lenses she'd ever looked through. She knew she'd take some heat because they weren't standard bureau issue, but she didn't care; she liked them and loved the way they fit.

As her eyes adjusted to the light, the view from the top of the building came into focus. It couldn't be described as spectacular, but it did offer a bird's-eye perspective of the crowded 405 Freeway traffic directly below inching along slowly in both directions north and south. To the west, lush trees surrounded the hillsides of upscale Brentwood. The southern view offered nothing but industrial office buildings and smog; same to the east, except the eastern buildings reached higher and higher, as if trying to find a way up through the smog. Looking north just over Wilshire Boulevard was the historical Los Angeles National Cemetery, which borders the beautiful UCLA campus to its east. That's why Fields came up to the roof. A history buff with a photographic memory, she loved gazing out over the impeccably manicured grounds, perfect rows of pure white headstones and trees. Spotting a grounds man driving a lawnmower, she wished she could smell the fresh-cut grass but knew there was no chance. When inside her office, surrounded by steel, glass, and concrete, all harshly bathed in fluorescent lights, this rooftop spot was her temporary sanctuary amidst the insanity that is the City of Fallen Angels.

Unless the helipad had incoming traffic, there was never anyone else on the roof. She was alone with the dozen rooftop surveillance cameras, which she could give a shit about.

From her perch, she could make out the granite obelisk situated in the San Juan Hill area of the 114-acre cemetery grounds that reads: "In Memory of the Men Who Offered Their Lives in Defense of Their Country." Fields found it intriguing that there was no date of dedication, nor that any donor information had ever been located for this pillar of a tribute. The cemetery was dedicated in 1889. She could imagine the horse-drawn wagons, wooden scuffling, ropes, and pulleys that were required to transport and erect such a monument. It made her smile that whoever had thought of the tribute never wanted any personal recognition. The fact was that someone had gone to extreme lengths to remain anonymous, something that would never happen today, she thought sadly, not with everyone looking to go viral with their selfies.

She'd walked the grounds on numerous occasions when she needed time to think through a case without any distractions. One afternoon she'd come across an unusual burial. Returning to the office, she did some research, discovering that the practice is now prohibited, making this national cemetery unique in that it has two such burial sites. Discovering the details on those two final resting places endeared her to the place forever.

The first was a dog by the name of Old Bonus, whom after his master was buried wouldn't leave the side of his master's grave. Bonus became an adopted pet of the caretakers who resided on the property and was buried next to his master when he passed. But it was the second discovery that brought Fields to her knees—the final resting place of a World War II war-dog named Blackout. Wounded in the Pacific theatre, Blackout was buried with her handler: George Lewis Oshier, Cook, US Navy Sergeant, US Marine Corps.

When Fields initially stumbled on Section 99, Row 2, Grave 99 and read the engraving, she broke down in tears, kneeling on the hallowed ground at the foot of these fallen heroes. A soldier and his dog killed in action and buried together. She could only imagine what they'd endured together and how they'd remained loyal to one another to the very end. Through her tears, she looked out over the rows and rows of white headstones, thinking to herself, *There's got to be a better way to run the world.*

Her vivid imagination as to what Blackout and George meant to each other slowly evolved into becoming something she drew on every day to get her through the job, replacing her long-lost reason for joining the bureau that she could somehow make a difference.

She pulled her phone out of her packet and dialed.

"Steel," she said, hearing his voice, "it's me, Agent Fields."

The pause on the other end of the line threw her for a moment. Then, "It's good to hear your voice. I've been thinking about you."

That made her smile. "We should talk. Do you have any time?"

"I'm out-of-pocket right now," he told her, "but we should have this wrapped up in a couple of days. Can it wait?"

"Of course," she told him instantly. *I don't know if I can,* she thought to herself before telling him, "Nothing pressing. Just wanted to go over a few things from the other day."

"Roger," he said. "I'll give you a call as soon as we're back in."

"Sounds good."

"Fields?"

"Yeah?"

"Nice hearing your voice again."

"Likewise."

After hanging up, Fields felt a twinge of disappointment in not getting to talk things over with him right then, but he'd told her he was undercover, and since it wasn't a pressing matter, it would have to wait. However, she couldn't help thinking about why the hell had she been sent down to Newport to begin with, and then there was that ridiculous interview with her chief. Her instincts told her something wasn't right, so she'd headed to the rooftop hoping it might help her stumble onto something.

Ever since those knuckleheads fucked up in Cartagena during the Presidents' Summit back in April 2012, the bullshit had been flowing downhill so thick through the halls of Washington that people were doing tap-dances on top of their desks trying to keep from getting buried. How a handful of experienced agents could get caught with their dicks hanging out like that was beyond her, but they had, and now, years later, it was still a huge deal, even though the department's damage control PR team had spun the mainstream media off the scent, but internally it was still a shit storm. When Defense Secretary Leon Panetta announced to the world that "We let the boss down," it had started the ball rolling, and the shit river hadn't stopped flowing since, with everyone ducking for cover trying to cover their ass.

Of the twelve agents involved in the Cartagena incident, the service declared that only three of the twelve implicated agents would stay with the agency. Of the three remaining with the service, one had been stripped of his security clearance, and the other two had been cleared of any wrongdoing. Of the nine agents leaving the service, one retired, two were fired, and six resigned. Twelve additional United States Armed Forces members who were on support duty at the time in Columbia had their security clearances suspended by the Pentagon.

Funniest thing about it, Fields thought to herself when she had first read the docket, was a sidebar that the Columbians were amused by the entire ordeal. When the call girl at the center of the whole fiasco got stiffed, she turned the agent into the local police, not knowing he was an agent. She said in an interview later on W-Radio that had she known she would have never said a word, especially given the fact, one of the other agents had ended up paying her anyway.

63

As part of the fallout, the Secret Service imposed new rules that prohibit agents from visiting "non-reputable establishments" or consuming alcohol ten hours before starting a shift. *They might as well close up shop now,* Fields thought to herself. She didn't know an agent that didn't drink. In addition, while on assignment, strict restrictions as to whom is allowed into their hotel rooms had also been initiated.

Another banner day for law enforcement she thought, *but nothing compared to the disgusting crap that has been going on at the top of the heap since the beginning of time.* She thought back over key details of just a few cases that came to mind while still gazing over the endless rows of white headstones from the rooftop.

January 21, 1998: *Washington Post* reporter Michael Isikoff exposed the Lewinsky scandal between then President Bill Clinton and a twenty-two-year-old White House intern, Monica Lewinsky. The news of this extramarital affair and the resulting investigation led to impeachment proceedings against President Clinton by the House of Representatives for perjury and lying about the affair under oath.

Spearheading the impeachment hearings was Representative Henry Hyde (R-IL), who was married and having an affair with a married woman during the proceedings. Representative Newt Gingrich (R-GA), leading the impeachment proceedings against President Clinton for perjury, was himself having an affair at the time with his own intern while married to his second wife.

Representative Robert Livingston (R-LA) called for President Clinton's resignation before his own extramarital affairs were discovered.

Representative Bob Barr (R-GA), had an affair while married and had been the first lawmaker in either chamber to call for Presidents Clinton's resignation.

Dan Burton (R-IN), a combative critic of President Clinton's affair, later admitted that he had fathered a child out of wedlock.

Helen Chenoweth-Hage (R-ID) aggressively called for President Clinton's resignation and later admitted to her own six-year affair with a married rancher.

Representative Ken Calvert (R-CA), champion of the Christian Coalition, was quoted as saying, "We can't forgive what occurred between the president and Lewinsky." Calvert himself was later arrested for soliciting a prostitute for oral sex in his car.

All of this took place before the 1998 midterm elections—and the American voters honestly don't think politics, sex, and money go hand in hand?

February 12, 1999: Following a twenty-one-day trial by the United States Senate after impeachment by the US House of Representatives, President Clinton was acquitted on all impeachment charges of perjury and obstruction of justice—just seventeen votes short of being removed from office.

Fields could only shake her head as case after case rambled through her mind.

November 23, 2012: Robert Decheine, a senior advisor to the Obama campaign in 2008, chief of staff to Representative Steve Rothman (D-NJ), was arrested on a felony count of sexual solicitation of a minor in a joint operation involving the Montgomery County Police, the Montgomery County State's Attorney's Office, the Maryland State Police, and the FBI. Gaithersburg Police made the arrest in a parking lot after Decheine solicited sex from an undercover officer posing as a fifteen-year-old girl.

Field kept asking herself, *What am I not seeing? Why is the Bureau suddenly getting involved with local prostitution cases?*

2008: Senator Brandon Edwards (D-NC) had his presidential campaign undercut when he admitted to an extramarital affair with actress Rielle Hunter, which produced a child during the time his wife was dying of cancer.

How fucking low can these scumbags go?

November 17, 2006: Brian J. Doyle (R), deputy press secretary of Homeland Security, was sentenced to five years in prison for seducing who he thought was a fourteen-year-old girl on the internet. She was actually a sheriff's deputy.

Score one for the good guys.

1987: Senator Gary Hart (D-CO), while seeking the Democratic nomination for president, was photographed in a compromising position with model Donna Rice and had to drop out of the race.

Robert L. Leggett (D-CA) acknowledged that he fathered two illegitimate children by a Congressional secretary whom he supported financially. He then had an affair with another woman who was an aide to Speaker Carl Albert.

1976: Allan Howe (D-UT) was arrested for soliciting two undercover police officers posing as prostitutes.

1976: Congressman Wayne Hays' (D-OH) career was ended when Elizabeth Ray admitted on record her actual job duties were providing Hays with sexual favors. She was quoted as saying, "I can't type. I can't file. I can't even answer the phone."

1974: Wilbur Mills (D-AR) was found intoxicated with stripper Fanne Foxe. He was re-elected but resigned after giving an intoxicated press conference from Foxe's burlesque house dressing room.

1964: Walter Jenkins (D), a longtime aide to President Lyndon B. Johnson, was arrested for having homosexual sex in a YMCA bathroom.

1962-63: President John F. Kennedy (D) was linked to a number of extramarital affairs, including an eighteen-month affair with intern Mimi Alford, as reported in an interview with Meredith Vierra on *Rock Center*, February 9, 2012.

The 1998 book *A Very Private Woman: The Life and Unsolved Murder of Presidential Mistress Mary Meyer* by Nina Burliegh creates more questions than answers, but it is most telling in its description about the nature of power and the manner by which it is achieved.

1921-1923: President Warren Harding (R), while married, had affairs with several women.

1884: President Grover Cleveland (D), a bachelor, paid child support to Moria Crofts Halpin, even though he may not have been the father of her son. Halpin had sexual relations with a number of men, including Cleveland's close friend and future father-in-law, Oscar Folsom, for whom the child was named.

Talk about some twisted shit.

1802: President Thomas Jefferson was accused of fathering the children of his slave, Sally Hemmings, in the published articles of James Challender.

Two-hundred years of lying, cheating politicians, Field thought to herself. *All cock-sucking assholes passing the very laws telling us how we should live our lives.*

While mentally playing back her little highlight reel, slowly, subtle fragments started to drift into place. If one thing over the years history has taught the scumbag politician: don't get caught. *This case isn't about prostitution. It's about the powers that be and maintaining their status, about staying in power. In essence,* Fields surmised, *if this is indeed the case, it reduces the agency to being nothing more than surveillance watchdogs for the elite.*

"Fuck that," Fields said out loud. "Someone's pulling the strings on this circus act, and I'm going to find out who."

Fields had stumbled onto the tip of an iceberg with an extremely violent history that was in the midst of repeating itself.

Chapter 6

The *New York Times,* October 16, 1907:

New York Stock Exchange Crashes
    Catastrophic financial crisis could collapse US financial system. Banks lock their doors as panic sweeps the nation.

***

Nelson W. Aldrich, head of the Senate Finance Committee, establishes and chairs a commission to investigate the crisis and "provide the nation with a safer, more flexible and stable monetary financial system" in order to prevent another meltdown from ever happening again.

***

December 23, 1913: The Federal Reserve Act is signed into law by President Woodrow Wilson.

***

The Federal Reserve is not a bank, nor does it have any reserves. What it does have is the exclusive power to "coin money" and authorize production of legal tender for the United States of America.

At the Fed's direction, the United States Department of the Treasury physically prints and mints said legal tender—100 percent of which is owned by the US Federal Government, less a "small" statutory dividend of 6 percent that is paid to the Federal Reserve for its "management services," courtesy of the United States taxpayers—on average, a management fee of a little over four billion dollars annually.

The Federal Reserve is composed of a presidentially appointed seven-member Board of Governors. It consists of twelve regional facilities located in "major" financial hubs throughout the country, which were determined in fiercely fought political battles in the halls of numerous privately-owned banks and "advisory councils." Within the Federal Reserve, the Federal Open Market Committee (FOMC) is responsible for setting monetary policy. The FOMC consists of all members of the Federal Reserve's Board of Governors and the twelve regional bank presidents, although only five bank presidents may vote at any given time on any given issue.

The Federal Reserve is a completely independent organization. It is a system of money created by bankers for the benefit of the bankers. The American people like to think that we have a democratic system, but there is absolutely nothing democratic about the Federal Reserve. Unelected, unaccountable central planners from a private central institution run our financial system and manage our economy.

***

"The Fed's monetary policy decisions do not require approval of the president or either of the legislative branches. These motherfuckers don't answer to anyone," Fields went on, explaining to Steel.

69

"But what does all this financial shit have to do with our case?" Steel asked.

"You're a smart guy," she challenged, "connect the dots."

They were seated opposite one another, perched on top of hundred-year-old, sixteen-by-sixteen, rough-sewn beams secured atop barnacle-covered, concrete pilings that extended the land-based portion of the Blue Water Grill out over the waters of Newport Harbor. It was late afternoon, and there were only a few other patrons on the deck, allowing them to speak freely without concerns of being overheard.

"Sorry, Fields," he said, shaking his head. "I'm just a cop. I chase bad guys. I don't have a clue what you're alluding to with all this high finance. I'm lucky every month if I don't bounce any checks."

Fields chuckled. With her photographic memory, she knew the daily balance on every one of her accounts and credit cards to the penny. Her ease with numbers and obsession with keeping accurate accounting, coupled with her knowledge that every branch of the government was financially on the verge of collapse, was one of the reasons she'd started looking into the Federal Reserve and how it makes policies that affect the entire globe.

"You find that amusing?" Steel asked.

"I think it's cute," she said. "Badass cop bringing down bad guys, running the SI unit, and you can't balance your checkbook."

"I didn't say I couldn't. I just don't take the time."

"That's my point," Fields challenged again, looking Steel directly in the eyes.

"Riddles bore me," Steel said, coming off more defensive than intended. "They're a waste of time."

"Exactly my point," Fields explained. Steel just looked at her as she continued. "We're all so goddamned busy, working our asses off trying to make ends meet—kids, soccer, assignments whatever. Bottom line, we don't have time to think about this shit."

"And?"

"And that's by design."

"I'm still not following you. I'm trying, but I'm just not seeing your point. What's by design?"

"We're all working so hard, each of us focused on our own little world, trying to survive, to get through the day, that we don't have time to see or think about the bigger picture."

All Steel could do was shake his head.

"I'm talking about chasing the American dream."

"Okay . . . but what about it?"

"It's become nothing more than an illusion."

"Grant you that," Steel agreed. "Seems like no matter how hard I try, I can't seem to get ahead."

"Exactly," Fields glowed, thinking he'd gotten it.

"Thank God for credit cards," Steel added.

"No. No," Fields countered.

"I give up," Steel confessed.

Letting out a deep sigh, Fields asked him, "Please, this shit's important. I know it is."

"But?"

"But I need you to help me figure it out."

"I swear to God I'm trying, but nothing you're saying makes any sense."

"Okay, let me summarize what I've come up with so far in the simplest of terms, and if you're still not getting it, I promise we can talk about something else."

"I'm all ears."

Fields smiled in spite of how their conversation had gone thus far. "First, why is the agency involved? Why is the FBI investigating local prostitution? That's not what we do."

Steel nodded in agreement. "That's what I thought after I was told you guys were coming down. Made no sense at all."

"I agree," Fields confirmed. "I've been asking myself the same question: why? I was coming up blank. Until my boss called me in the other day, the day I called you, and asked for my personal assessment of your case."

"No shit?" Steel asked, now fully attentive, leaning in, knowing full well how off the charts that type of question was from a superior within law enforcement.

"No shit," Fields confirmed. "I left his office convinced now more than ever that something was up. It just smelled like a rat. After I thought about it for a while, I called you."

Steel smiled. "Then let's see if maybe there's some way I can help you figure it out."

Fields summarized their conversation to this point, adding, "In every case, I'm always looking, as I'm sure you are, for a common thread, anything that connects things, even if it's the most far-fetched, random, lowest common denominator, anything that links the pieces together."

"And?"

"We're the perps."

"Please . . ." Steel begged, more with his eyes than words.

"We are. All of us that work for a living."

Fields continued, "As diverse as we all are, as different as all of our lives are, as diverse as any jobs in the country can be, from Uber drivers to brain surgeons, it doesn't matter. The common thread, the link, is the fact that we're all working, striving to make better lives for ourselves, for our kids, our loved ones; it doesn't matter, we all share one common denominator."

"And that is?"

"We all pay taxes."

A hot mess. What a waste, Steel thought to himself. *She's a wacko with a gun and a badge.* "So what?" he asked politely, thinking, *It's time to end this conversation*, but stating "People have been paying taxes since the beginning of time."

"Not entirely true, but for the sake of argument, let's say you're right."

"So, what do taxes have to do with prostitution, other than they don't pay any."

"Tax evasion isn't the issue. Not even close." Field shook her head.

"Then if it's not about evasion, what is it?"

"Making sure the system continues to perpetuate itself," Field answered him. "A system designed to sustain itself through thick and thin, through war and peace, good times and bad, it doesn't matter. The system has been perfected over the years to run no matter what."

"And how has that been accomplished?"

"I don't know," Fields answered honestly. "But I do know that everywhere you look, the nurturing illusion is that if you work hard, someday you can actually get the carrot. Stories of self-made billionaires are everywhere, Zuckerberg, Jack Dorsey/ Twitter, Uber's Travis Kalanick—hell, even Brady and LeBron are practically billionaires."

"Work hard and the American dream can be yours in all its living glory," Steel added.

"Basically, reducing the vast majority of us to a little more than meaningless worker bees in the grand scheme of things."

"Which is what exactly?" Steel asked.

Fields paused, looking him in the eye again before saying, "To make sure there will always be a perpetual base in this country that's striving for a better life—earning, consuming and most importantly, paying taxes."

"Hold on," Steel challenged. "You can't be serious."

"Serious as a heart attack."

A silence settled over their table. Steel was reviewing, trying to absorb the full spectrum of what Fields was covering. Other than reading about the cheaters the SEC and Justice Department had nailed carrying out the fine Wall Street tradition of making a mint with insider trading, he'd never given it a second thought.

"So, you're telling me assholes like Donald Johnson, Milken, and Ivan Boesky are changing the course of history through their insider trading?"

Fields laughed. "Not at all. Not even close. That's like thinking Martha Stewart going to prison for her little ImClone stock deal matters. Wall Street is just an open market, a place where people do business. There is always going to be cheating and lying." She paused. "Think bigger. Think globally, seemingly random events that affect entire countries, even entire continents . . . the world."

He was aware of conspiracy theories, rumors about manipulating global markets, influencing vast power bases, changing world events, altering the course of history, but he thought it was all bullshit.

Fields waited patiently, watching every expression on his face processing the information.

"So, you're saying you think there are mysterious individuals out there wielding enough power to alter human events?"

"Article One, Section Eight of the Constitution states that the US Congress is the entity that has the sole authority to—and I quote—coin money, regulate the value thereof, unquote. So, tell me why the Federal Reserve is doing it."

Steel shrugged his shoulders.

Fields continued. "And it's not just here in the US. That's why I said think bigger. There are Federal Reserves set up all over the world. In fact, all one hundred eighty-seven nations that belong to the IMF have a central bank. Are we really supposed to believe that this is all just some sort of a bizarre coincidence?"

"Okay, the more you talk, the more convinced I am that you're a whack job," he said, looking her in the eye. "How could global finance possibly connect to what looks to be no more than a well-managed floating brothel here in my little town?"

Fields' eyes met his. "That's why I'm reaching out to you."

"Why can't we keep it simple and just bust the bad guys?"

"That's exactly what I'm trying to do."

"By investigating the Federal Reserve?" Steel shook his head. "Honestly, you're certifiable. The goddamned president can't even get inside those hallowed halls."

"Steel, please, listen. Hear me out."

"I don't know if I can handle anymore."

"Please," she requested.

He nodded.

"I'm sorry. Sometimes I get caught up in the minute details," she said, looking into his eyes, making sure he wanted her to continue and that he hadn't in fact decided she was certifiable. She smiled before continuing, sensing she hadn't completely lost him yet. "Let me fill you in with a little bit of history, and if it doesn't start making sense after that," she added, "then I promise, I'll shut up and never talk about it again."

"Fire away," Steel said. "I'll try and keep up."

"Okay," she said excitedly. "Here's the Cliffs Notes' version. About a hundred years ago, a few of the wealthiest men in the country got together, in total secrecy, and set the entire thing up."

"What thing? The Federal Reserve?"

"Yep."

"Who exactly?"

"J. D. Rockefeller Jr., John Pierpont Morgan—"

"*The* J. P. Morgan?" Steel interrupted.

"Yep, the original kingpin of Wall Street, along with Rockefeller and the most powerful political figure of the day, Senator Nelson Aldrich, who lorded over the nation's financial matters."

"You're telling me three men set up the entire Federal Reserve?"

"Correct-a-mundo," Fields said, adding, "I've started thinking of them as the Elite Three."

"That's insane. There's no way," Steel asserted.

"With the communications we have today, for sure, no way they could have pulled it off. But back a hundred years ago, think about it. How did people get information?"

"Good point. But why the cloak and dagger?"

"These guys were creating the most exclusive club in the world. They knew if word got out, they would have been hung. Keeping their identities completely secret, Aldrich and assistant secretary of the Treasury Department at the time, a guy named A. P. Andrews, discretely invited a handpicked group of prominent bankers, financial experts from Wall Street's upper crust, and to round out the field, a few select economic scholars from the country's top universities, to attend a conference off the coast of the small Georgia port town of Brunswick on a private resort owned by Morgan, known as Jekyll Island."

"How do you know all this shit?" Steel interrupted.

"I'm a history buff. It's all public information. Anyone can look it up," Fields told him. "But listen, this is where it starts getting good. The meeting was set up under the ruse of it being a duck-hunting excursion. When in reality, our Elite Three were laying the foundation for restructuring and taking over control of America's entire banking system."

"This is fucking hard to believe," Steel objected.

"I know," Fields assured him, "but it's all fact, available for anyone through the Freedom of Information Act. B. C. Forbes, founder of *Forbes* magazine, wrote about it and, I'm quoting him here, 'Picture a party of the nation's greatest bankers stealing out of New York on a private railroad car, under cover of darkness, stealthily riding hundreds of miles south, embarking on a mysterious launch, sneaking onto an island deserted by all but a few servants, living there for ten days under such rigid secrecy that the names of not one of the men was ever once mentioned, lest the servants learn the identity and disclose to the world this the strangest, most secret expedition in the history of American finance. I am not romancing. I am giving to the world, for the first time, the real story of how the famous Aldrich Currency Report, the foundation of our currency system, was written.'"

Steel was speechless.

Ignoring his bewilderment, Fields continued, "On December 23, 1913, the sitting Congress passed the Federal Reserve Act."

"Two days before Christmas?" Steel asked.

"No coincidence there. And besides the precise timing, it was colder than shit that day in Washington. President Woodrow Wilson immediately signed the bill, and the legislation was enacted into law that same day, December 23, 1913, creating the Federal Reserve System. Charles Hamlin became the Fed's first chairman, with none other than J. P. Morgan's personal deputy, Benjamin Strong, becoming the first president of the Federal Reserve Bank of New York, the most important regional bank in the system, which along with the presidency earned him a permanent seat on the Federal Open Market Committee. Virtually overnight, the Elite Three took control of the country's entire banking system. And do you want to know what else?"

Steel just shook his head.

"Get this," Fields told him. "The first ever federal income tax was also introduced at the same time."

"What are you saying? That before they set up the Fed there wasn't any income tax?"

"Nope. Not a dime."

"You gotta be shitting me."

"Afraid not," Fields confirmed. "Up until that moment, the government having the right to tax the income a man made from the sweat of his brow was completely foreign to Americans."

"I'm blown away."

"You should be. These guys didn't miss a thing. When you detach and look at it from a distance, it's pure genius."

Steel thought he'd pretty much seen it all, but hearing this blew him away. "I don't know what to say."

"I know," Fields agreed, "I feel the same way. Mind numbing it's so overwhelming."

Steel nodded in agreement. "So, what are you thinking all this has to do with our case?"

"I don't know," Fields admitted, thinking out loud, "but staying focused on just the facts, as unbelievable as they are, the common denominators are that money and power equals control."

"I still can't make the connection between the little escort service we're investing, you, the agency, and everything you've been telling me."

"I know," Fields admitted. "The whole thing is overwhelming."

"A tad," Steel answered sarcastically.

"A little more backstory," Fields told him, "and you'll have all the facts."

Steel nodded.

"Once you've heard it all, then you can tell me I'm out of my frickin' mind and to take a hike."

"Don't count on it."

That made Fields smile before she continued. "While attending Brown, Rockefeller studied Karl Marx's *Das Kapital*.

The Kapital is a critique of a political economy. In summary, it states the ultimate success of capitalism is achieved through the exploitation of labor."

Seeing the blank stare on Steel's face, she smiled again. "Guessing history wasn't one of your strong suits in school."

"That obvious?"

"Exploitation of labor is a fancy way of saying low-paid workers are the ultimate source of profit."

"Why? Because they do all the work?"

"No, because they actually create the product by performing the manual labor required to build it."

"Build what?" Steel interrupted.

"It doesn't matter, whatever, anything, it doesn't matter. The value of low-paid workers lies in the fact that the employer owns all rights to all the products they build, the profits, because the employer owns the productive capital assets or means of production. Which, get this, are legally protected by law through property rights. So long as the employer is producing capital rather than commodities, like the actual goods the low-paid workers are producing, then they, the low-paid workers, are continually reproducing the economic conditions for which they labor and have no rights to the profits earned therein." Fields paused. "It's a rigged game."

"Perpetuating the rat race?" Steel offered lamely.

"Basically. But here's the kicker." Fields couldn't wait to tell Steel the most amazing part of this entire ordeal.

"I'm all ears."

"At the same time Rockefeller and Morgan established the Federal Reserve, Rockefeller, on his own, through the Rockefeller Foundation, created an insurance policy to guarantee their newly crafted banking system would never be challenged."

"How?"

"He created an organization called the American General Education Board, which," Fields continued, "provided the vast majority of funding for schools across the entire country."

"Okay. So?"

"While funding and promoting the state-controlled public-school movement," Fields asked sarcastically, "how could anyone object to better schools? Right?" Fields continued without pausing. "The fucker was a flat-out genius because, get this, in addition to providing all funding, the General Education Board set the curriculum guidelines for what subjects were to be taught. If any school wanted funding, it was required to teach only the curriculum the board wanted."

"Which was?"

"Reading, writing, and arithmetic—but most importantly teaching children to be obedient, reliable, productive citizens."

"Seriously?"

"But what's inconceivable today," Fields continued, "is that our nation's entire school system back in the early part of the twentieth century was completely controlled by industry, a tool industrial moguls used as a form of governance. Education back then wasn't anything even near a resemblance of the schools and institutions of higher learning we have today."

"I'd say," Steel agreed.

"And," Fields continued excitedly, "at the same time, the federal government mandated, for the first time in our country's history, that all children must attend public school, and, at the direction of Rockefeller's board, the young minds be taught the fundamental skills of reading, writing, and arithmetic in order to go forth into the workplace and be good, productive citizens."

"You mean," Steel said, connecting the dots, "good employees."

"Exactly," Fields said. "We are, and have been for generations, been taught from day one how to be good employees."

Steel slowly shook his head.

"For over a hundred years, the Rockefellers, along with the a few of the other financially elite, have been molding society, starting grade one, by funding compulsory state schooling and—this is the ultimate creed—declaring that no classes about finances or monetary systems ever be taught in America's public-school systems."

"That's bullshit," Steel objected. "What about all the business classes, accounting and bookkeeping? I know those classes were available back when I was in school."

"Honestly, Steel," Fields challenged him, "what does knowing how to keep a ledger or balance a set of books have to do with finances?"

Steel didn't answer.

"So," she continued, "that left only the few select youth from only the wealthiest families—the Rockefellers, Morgans, Rothschilds, Carnegies, Vanderbilts, Hearsts, to name a few—destined for being educated and groomed in higher finances, all compliments of the Carnegie Rockefeller Foundation."

Steel was totally focused, glued to her every word.

"The director of charity for the Rockefeller Foundation, Frederick T. Gates, wrote, 'In our dream, the people yield themselves, with perfect docility, to our molding hand.'"

Steel shook his head. "It's hard to imagine how anything like this could have even transpired without people going nuts."

"Oh, a few did," she said, "or at least tried. In 1914, Gates was challenged in a resolution by the National Education Association, and I'm quoting again, 'We view with alarm the activity of the Carnegie and Rockefeller Foundations, agencies not in any way responsible to the people, in their efforts to control the policies of our states' educational institutions. To fashion after their conception, and to standardize our courses of study, and to surround the institutions with conditions which menace true academic freedom and defeat the primary purpose of democracy, as heretofore preserved, inviolate in our common schools and universities.'"

Fields was livid. "They squashed him like a tomato. Can't you see? They fixed the game."

"Seems like it," Steel acknowledged.

"They thought of the masses as nothing more than worker ants, knowing they could be best managed and controlled not by teaching them how to think for themselves, but in reality the opposite." Fields paused. "For over a hundred years, generation after generation of American children have been taught—from the first grade on—good children obey; they do as they're told."

Steel nodded in agreement as Fields continued, "Do not question authority, work hard, and be thankful for what you have."

"And if you follow all the rules," Steel finished her thought for her, "you'll be rewarded with a gold star."

Fields summarized, "The smartest continue their education, becoming doctors and lawyers, businessmen, professionals, even cops, firemen, teachers, nurses, whatever; it doesn't matter." Fields paused, letting the reality of the situation continue to sink in. "No matter how hard we work or how much we make, we're paying with our lives to play a game we can't win. The rich keep getting richer, while the rest of us toil in our fields of our choice because, in mass, we continually reproduce the economic conditions under which we labor." Fields could only shake her head in surrender.

"If this is all true, it's genius," Steel murmured, "pure fucking genius."

"No one ever accused those guys of being stupid."

"The rich keep getting richer as the rest of us toil in a fixed game," Steel said, "a system instilled and institutionalized into the minds of generation after generation of Americans since the beginning of modern education."

"And almost every single one of us buy into it hook, line, and sinker," Fields added.

"The American dream: of the people, by the people, and for the people."

Fields nodded. "Only it's of the few, by the few, and for the few. Or perhaps even more accurately stated: of the money, by the money, and for the money."

Fields reached inside her purse. Pulling out a dollar bill, she handed it to him. "Look at the back. The words around the pyramid."

Steel did as she instructed.

Annuit Coeptis," Fields said, "Latin for 'Providence Favors our Undertakings,' and *Novus Ordo Seclorum*, Latin for 'New Order of the Ages.' Since 1935, these words appear on every dollar bill the Feds have ever printed."

Steel stared at the dollar bill he was holding.

"Think about it," Fields offered. "The reason the markets don't give a shit when the president says anything about the economy but go fucking crazy whenever Bernanke opens his mouth is because they know the Feds have all the power." She paused. "Yet, in spite of all this, we believe, since it's been maliciously, systematically drilled into our collective consciousness since day one, that we live and breathe in a free democratic system, while in reality there's not a goddamn democratic thing about the Federal Reserve. The unelected, unaccountable, untouchables. The elites—extremely intelligent, ruthless individuals—are manipulating the world's economies from totally secure, private, centralized locations, operating in the open yet beyond the reach of the law or government, protected by the very laws they wrote when creating the thing a hundred years ago."

"What I can't wrap around," Steel questioned, "is if any part of what you're saying is even remotely true. How have they possibly been able to maintain a system, created as you say by the elite for the elite, without someone in our government figuring it out and shutting them down?"

"I don't know, but something's going on. Something's got 'em worried."

"How do you figure?"

"Why else would they be pulling out all the stops?"

"What do you mean?"

"Don't know for sure. I'm still trying to string all the pieces together, but back in 1909, a guy by the name of Alinsky was born to poor Russian immigrants, just another kid on the streets of Chicago. By the time he was in his teens, he hated the system, the cops, the government, big business—basically blaming everything good he saw around him for his poverty. Turns out he was a pretty intelligent kid and a history buff," Fields added.

"Okay, so what does he have to do with all this?"

"The difference is that he hated this country; I love it."

"So now it's personal? You and this guy Alinsky?"

"Damn right. I told you, I'm a history freak, a complete nerd when it comes to our heritage. I love reading biographies and profiles of influential men and women in our history, and every once in a while someone jumps off the pages. I'm still just trying to find all the dots," Fields confessed. "Connecting them is another thing all together."

"Go on," Steel encouraged her. "Please. I'm fascinated."

"Long story short, Alinsky began publishing pamphlets about the horrific working conditions in the factories and living conditions in the ghettos of Chicago. In so many words, accusing the Feds of doing exactly what they'd set out to do. He was one of the first to start figuring out ways to organize the poor, the low-paid labor—or the masses, as the elite call them. As his flock grew, it slowly, ever so slowly, started to transform into a very vocal and relatively forceful mass."

"Not exactly part of the elite's plan?"

"Precisely."

"So besides pissing these guys off, what happened?"

"He wrote a thing he called Rules of Radicals."

"And?"

"And as it turns out, a couple of dots connected when I read that Alinsky's Rules for Radicals was the bible for another community organizer growing up in Chicago, a young man by the name of Obama."

"Give me the Cliffs Notes," Steel asked.

"It's a how-to for have-nots on how to change the world from what it is to what they believe it should be."

"How specifically?"

"Basically, sneak up behind them, reach around, grab their balls, and yank as hard as you can."

Steel nodded, finishing her sentence. "And their hearts and minds will follow."

Fields, nodding now, said, "Like the entire system, it's frightening in its simplicity."

"I could use something simple right now," Steel told her.

"This is anything but, trust me." Fields told him.

"Go on."

"Here's Alinsky in the simplest of terms. He says that in order to create a socialist state, the government has to A) control healthcare. Control healthcare and you control the masses. B) increase poverty, because destitute people lack the will to fight back. Whatever meager possessions they do have, they're receiving from government programs, so they aren't about to bite the hand that's feeding them. C) keep creating ways to increase taxes on those that work. Tax 'em until you break them. Take away their money and you minimize what power they may have had. And D) remove an individual's ability to defend themselves."

"Take away their guns?" Steel interrupted.

"Yep, and if you do all the above, you're on your way to creating a welfare-dependent society. Control the masses, as you so eloquently stated, and you've got 'em by the balls."

"Jesus," Steel said, shaking his head. "This is starting to sound real."

"No shit," Fields said, nodding in agreement. "Alinsky added systematic education, which we've already covered, control what young minds are taught in school, control information and control what people read—the press."

"This guy Alinsky wrote all this back in the twenties?"

Fields nodding yes, continued, "Remove prayer from the schools. Destroy the people's belief in their God." And finally she said, "Divide and conquer. Constantly fuel class warfare, breed hatred and social unrest, always pointing the finger at and blaming those with money."

"Not a hard sell."

"Not at all. The impoverished eat this shit up. It's easy to blame someone else for your problems. It takes away any personal responsibility," Fields said bluntly. "The greater the distance between the haves and have nots, the greater the discontent, the more volatile the social climate, the easier it is to continue increasing taxes on the wealthy with the overwhelming support from the majority poor."

"That's flat-out frightening when you put it that way."

"No shit," Fields confirmed. "And get this, Hillary did her college thesis on Alinsky. She and Obama both think the asshole walked on water."

"We're fucked," Steel said, shaking his head.

"Pretty much," Fields confirmed. "This country is sitting smack dab in the middle of the tracks with two freight trains running full speed towards a head-on collision."

"You mean," Steel asked, "the Feds and the White House?"

"Basically, depending on which party is in office, but it's goes much deeper than that," Fields said softly without looking up. "Obama got himself elected without the support of the Feds who, up until he got into office, basically had control over those in that office for the past hundred years, maybe with the exception of JFK, who they just ended up killing. Given Obama is the most paranoid president we've ever had, completely isolated twenty-four by seven, with ten times more CIA protection than any other president in history, they simply haven't been able to get to him."

"Now you're talking crazy," Steel confronted her.

"Am I?" she questioned him. "Alinsky was dead less than a year after he published that paper."

Steel paused before asking, "How?"

"Massive heart attack while standing on a street corner in Carmel."

"Any evidence of foul play?" Steel asked, realizing how lame that sounded as it came out, knowing if enough money wanted a killing to look like natural causes there wouldn't be any evidence.

She just looked at him.

"Sorry," he said sheepishly. "But you have to admit, this all sounds too bizarre to be real."

She looked up. "Maybe," she confessed. "Maybe I've just been making myself nuts with all this." Her gaze returned to the table.

Steel reached out and took her hand. After a long pause, he told her, "I'm trying to wrap my head around everything you're saying."

She looked up hopefully.

Steel met her probing look and continued in a calm voice. "Can I sit here and tell you I believe it all or not?" he said, slowly shaking his head. "Honestly, I can't. It's an interesting perspective on things, that's for damn sure." Pausing again, he continued, "But again, I have to ask, what's the connection between all this and the FBI caring about a few douchebags paying for sex?"

"Throughout history, men, good men," Fields told him, pausing without looking up, "have been ruined by following their dicks into places they shouldn't."

"Nature of the beast. Unfortunately, most men can't help it," Steel answered honestly. "God knows I've screwed things up more than once."

"From the tone in your voice, I'm guessing you've paid a price," Fields said.

Steel nodded in agreement, meeting her eyes.

"What I'm trying to figure out—and by the way," she said, pausing, "thank you for listening to all this." Steel nodded again but remained silent. "If we can figure out how the elite power brokers have been able to manipulate everything, basically our entire government, for a hundred years, then maybe, just maybe, we can find an answer."

"To what?" Steel asked blatantly.

Fields continued her train of thought. "If the American people ever even remotely understood how the Fed works, they'd be screaming to have it abolished. Think back over the past few elections. I can name a dozen candidates whose extramarital affairs suddenly, out of nowhere, at a critical point in their campaigns, surfaced and killed their chances."

"They're all scumbags, as far as I'm concerned," Steel added.

"Most are, and that's precisely what the elite want us to think. Throughout history, the vast majority of politicians have proven to be nothing more than greedy scumbags, but not all of them. Can you name the last great American hero who was in office?"

Steel just shook his head and said lamely, "John Wayne."

"I wish," she said, smiling, "only he was smart enough not to ever run. Maybe Colin Powell." Fields paused, thinking to herself. "But something changed his mind. After a lifetime of service, at a time when his star was shining the brightest, he just slipped out of sight. I know there are a few individuals out there, honest men and women who are trying to make a difference, but unfortunately, those are the ones getting trampled."

"By whom?" Steel asked.

"I wish I knew," Fields answered flatly. "What I'm trying to figure out right now is the how. If we can figure out how all these sexual scandals suddenly surface with such perfect timing, then maybe we might find a clue as to who's pulling the strings."

"The media?"

"No way," Fields rebutted. "Okay, maybe once in a while a relentless investigative reporter will uncover something on their own, but the vast majority of the time the media is being spoon fed leads. Remember, control what the people know, what they read, what they watch and listen to, and when. Someone is behind all this."

"You think it's the Federal Reserve?"

Fields nodded, adding, "Maybe. Maybe not. I don't know. Maybe not directly, but somehow they're involved."

"I'm sorry, but you're out of your fucking mind."

"You're right," she admitted. "If I uttered a word of this at work, I'd be gone in a heartbeat." Fields shook her head, trying to clear out all the data she'd been spewing. "I don't have a single thread of evidence, nothing; it's all spec. But, Steel, the history is there. It's right here in front of us in black and white. I just haven't been able to get through enough of it to put it all together."

"I'll give you the history is compulsive, but it's just too surreal. Something like this going on for over a century, and no one's the wiser? Especially today, not with the internet and the Freedom of Information Act, I just don't think it's possible."

"The FOIA is bullshit," Fields countered. "There are nine exceptions legally protected from disclosure, and that doesn't include the special law enforcement exclusions. Any shit that's really important is untouchable. Trust me, I've tried. If I can't get to it, and I'm the fucking FBI, no one can." Feeling defeated, Fields sat there staring at the water. "Ever hear the term normalcy bias?"

"I know that one," Steel said, "or at least I think I do."

"This isn't a quiz," Fields rebutted, shaking her head, knowing she'd lost him.

"They talked about it in one of our training classes on domestic abuse," Steel added.

Fields turned away from the water and met his eyes again. "Yeah, read the files. About fifteen million women annually report that the first time their husbands, boyfriends, significant others, whomever, hit them, they simply couldn't believe it because they'd never been hit before. It paralyzes them, like deer in the headlights. Fear, denial. A combination, I don't know," Fields continued, shaking her head, "Sociology defines normalcy bias as the phenomenon of disbelieving one's situation when faced with grave and imminent danger."

Getting back on point, Steel asked, "So you're saying you think we've all been conditioned, or brainwashed, into some sort of mental state of being that causes us to underestimate both the possibility of something occurring and its possible effects."

"It's not brainwashing," Fields answered him. "The bias causes us to believe that things will always function the way they normally do. We're simply incapable of believing something like what I've been describing could occur. Because it has never happened before, then it never will." Pausing again, Fields added, "We want to believe the best. It's drilled into our DNA. We are the best country in the world. A proud, forgiving country. We love rooting for the underdogs and think everyone deserves a second chance, or at least three strikes, which is ridiculous. But we are the most optimistic people on the planet."

"The American dream," Steel added.

"So long as no one ever gets close to discovering the truth, or any fraction of it. If they do, the powers that be simply change direction, change the rules, or eliminate the threat altogether. It doesn't matter to them. No one outside their little club matters. We're all just working ants, chasing that American dream. The bottom line is there are no checks or balances. At first, I was fixated on just the Feds, but now," Fields paused again before saying it out loud, "I think we are in the middle of a power struggle that could very well destroy this country."

"Way over my pay grade," Steel told her, trying to lighten the load.

"The Feds never have been accountable to anyone, and now with the White House hiding behind national security, no one's accountable. Misinformation, misdirection is everywhere. It's rapid. I don't even trust my own boss. It's terrifying, to be honest with you."

Steel remained silent.

"Two powerful forces," Fields paused, "extremely powerful forces, secretive, with unlimited financial resources, intellectual geniuses, giants, squaring off with the fate of the county hanging in the balance."

"And from all you've told me, the ability to eliminate anyone that gets in their way without a trace."

"Pretty much sums up."

"So, what's your plan?"

"My plan?" Fields said, slowly shaking her head. "I don't have a clue." she replied, Looking Steel in the eye. "I was hoping you might have something."

Seeing the spark in her eyes made him smile. "How about we finish lunch and take a walk out on the pier? I think better when I'm moving."

"Me too," she answered.

***

Fields finished her seared ahi Caesar salad while Steel woofed down the last of his sautéed panko-crusted calamari steak. The half loaf of homemade sourdough bread had long ago disappeared. Being on duty, they'd both opted for the Grill's delicious Arnold Palmers, which they had refilled before heading over to the Newport pier.

Completed in 1889, the thousand-foot-long wooden pier originally connected Newport with the rest of the country by rail running through Orange, Riverside, and San Bernardino counties, then parallel with US Route 66. The pier was the hub of the Newport business district. Still located in the center of the Balboa Peninsula, the pier remains a popular spot for tourists.

The surf was down as Fields and Steel strolled past the makeshift shanty town of what remained of the Dory fishing fleet. A once thriving beachside fish camp that has been working the abundant, fish rich, local waters long before the pier was built, the colorfully painted wooden boats, fish shacks, and vendors selling their fresh offerings was a throwback to an era when a man in a wooden boat could make a living fishing the sea. During the fleet's peak, over thirty boats would line the pier daily, each piled high with various species of seasonal fresh fish, crab, abalone, and lobster, peddling the best the Pacific had to offer. Today as they walked by, only one lone boat had a few sorry-looking white fish laid out on top of a small pile of melting ice. A grey-bearded fisherman in torn overalls and a stained sweatshirt with the letters CAT across the front was fast asleep, arched back in an old wooden chair leaning against the side of his boat, a ragged faded baseball cap pulled down over his eyes.

"Changing times," Steel muttered quietly as they passed, having grown up in Newport.

"Makes you wonder," Fields offered.

"About?" Steel asked.

"How we spend our lives."

"Going deep are we?" Steel said, pausing while they continued walking towards the open sea. "Don't get me wrong," he told her, "I love what I do. Shit, it's the only thing I know how to do. But looking at that old fisherman got me to thinking is all."

"Me too," Fields offered openly, confessing, "I have been since I met you."

This drew a look from Steel, their eyes meeting again momentarily.

Fields confessed, "Department didn't send me down today. I took personal time." She paused again. "I wanted to see you."

Looking down at the worn wooden planks, Steel knew she wasn't referring to discussing the case, or *her insane notions*, he thought to himself. But there was something in her voice, the same something that he'd thought he'd caught a glimpse of in her eyes when they said goodbye after lunch at Billy's. He looked over at her, and their eyes met. Neither blinked. They'd both seen first-hand the horrible things people are capable of doing to one another, the hatred and violence. Neither was the least bit afraid to look deeply into another's soul. It was one of the moments in life that change people forever.

Without uttering another word, they saw what they each needed to see. Details and logistics would come later, but for right now, in this moment, it was all that mattered. The world around them dissolved. Their fingers entwined as they continued walking towards the end of the pier.

***

Back at headquarters, Steel called his team together. He told them he'd met with Agent Fields, leaving out all her speculation and personal stuff, explaining he wanted to tap into Grey and her little band of strawberries. Operation Grey Suit was born.

Chapter 7

Daniel Craig, Roger Moore, and Sean Connery, the best ever at playing the James Bond character, couldn't hold a candle against Todd Winfield, the quintessential real-life 007. *Innocently handsome,* Jewels thought to herself. Charm and confidence radiated from within the very core of his being. Clear, kind eyes and an inviting smile, he was as secure with himself as any man she'd ever met. She'd melted at his touch and, to her dismay, hadn't been able to get him out of her mind since their afternoon on the yacht. She had no intentions of doing anything about it, but he was the final straw in her decision to quit.

"I've had a good run, but it's time to get out," she murmured to herself.

It wasn't unusual to have clients request repeat performances. Jewels preferred her assignments to be new targets. Sequels were usually a bore. Her handler knew her propensities—as if she had any say in the matter—and respected her preferences. She knew she was nothing more than a handsomely paid gun for hire and fully accepted her roll. Since reaching her decision to quit, she'd actually been waiting for contact, so she could request a meeting with her handler. She wanted to tell him in person that she was done.

However, when he did reach out, she had to decipher the coded message twice to confirm she wasn't missing something. Presence: plus one, Samantha. Evening: formal. Event: Democratic fundraiser. Host: George Clooney. Location: Clooney's home, Hollywood Hills. Call time: 1800 (Hrs.). Meet: Todd Winfield, plus one. Special Guest: The president of the United States.

The first and last lines stopped her in her tracks. She'd never received a "plus one" assignment before. Not that she couldn't handle it, but seeing Samantha's name, followed by the last line, actually took her breath away.

She immediately Googled it. Sure as shit, a political fundraiser—$50,000 a head to rub elbows with the president at Clooney's sprawling Tudor mansion in the hills above mecca. TMZ was all over the event, posting Wolfgang Puck himself and his band of culinary artisans would be providing the finest food being served on the planet at the evening's biggest event.

Jewels kept her political views private and could care less about seeing the president, but the thought of being in the same room as Clooney, in the house he bought twenty years ago from one of her all-time favorite vocalists, Stevie Nicks, made the assignment an evening she couldn't resist, even though she'd decided she didn't ever need to see Todd again. Fearful she may have already inhaled a bit more of Mr. Winfield than she could handle, the last thing she wanted to do was fuel the coals still smoldering from their afternoon together. She knew she'd be playing with fire seeing him again. Complications didn't interest her. She needed more information.

She coded her handler. Questions: Set Meet.

The instant response: Spa, Tomorrow 1000 (Hrs.)

**

Jewels arrived at The Spa ten minutes ahead of schedule. She checked in, clearing protocols, but instead of being shown to her dressing room, she was ushered down a private hallway to another set of elevators. The hostess gave a retinal scan, palmed the recessed reader, and punched in a code, smiling at Jewels as the door instantly opened, reaching inside the door the hostess punched a second set of codes. She smiled again as she exited the elevator, leaving Jewels alone for the ride up to the top floor of The Spa. *Damn those twinkles*, she thought to herself, *with their little hard bodies, and they have access codes.*

Before today, she'd never been invited to the top floor. She was aware of her heart rate increasing as she ascended. The elevator slowed and stopped. The doors opened automatically, revealing a beautifully appointed reception room with floor-to-ceiling, tinted glass windows revealing spectacular views of the Pacific. Rich dark-mahogany wood perfectly complemented the massive glass panorama. There was no receptionist, just a beautiful spacious area with tastefully appointed, overstuffed chairs, low side tables and lamps pleasantly spaced around the room. No sooner had she stepped out of the elevator than one of the doors along the room's rear interior wall opened and her handler stepped out.

"Always a pleasure to see you, Ms. Jewels," he said warmly, approaching her with his hand outstretched. "You look as lovely as ever."

"Thank you," Jewels answered. Even though they'd worked together for almost two decades, they'd only met face to face on one previous occasion.

"Please have a seat," he said, gesturing to a pair of chairs near the windows. Once they were seated, he asked, "Is there anything you'd like? Coffee, tea, juice, perhaps a fresh pastry?"

"No, thank you." Jewels nodded politely, the formalities being so foreign to their normal coded messages. *European,*

Jewels thought to herself, surprised she hadn't realized that years ago. But how much information can you learn about someone through coded messages anyway? "I'm fine."

"Very well," he continued. "You have questions?"

Jewels nodded. Not sure where to start. "I do," she said politely, "and I apologize in advance for wasting any of your time due to my ignorance."

"Of course not, my darling. You have nothing to apologize for. You are anything but ignorant and never waste my time. You have been nothing but a pleasure to work with all these years, the consummate professional on every level." He smiled more to himself than at Jewels, adding, "If only there were more like you."

"Thank you," Jewels said sincerely. "I feel the same way about you."

"If I'm not mistaken," he asked, "this is the first time you've ever requested a meet like this?"

"It is," she confirmed. "Actually, there are a couple of issues I'd like to discuss."

"I'm all yours," he said pleasantly.

"First of all, the Clooney assignment sounds interesting, but the plus one?"

"That's totally understandable," he assured her in his warm voice. "We rarely, if ever, invite outsiders, but given the unique circumstances of this particular event, we decided things would flow more naturally if you actually were with your long-time, and I know very close and personal friend."

Jewels was shocked. *Is he actually asking me to bring Sam along as an escort? He's out of his mind.*

Anticipating the question, he added instantly. "Jewels, please, not in a million years would we ever request anything like what I assume you're thinking. I'm so sorry I wasn't clearer initially. Please accept my apologies for any concerns this has caused you."

Jewels nodded but didn't say anything.

"Mr. Winfield has a gentleman friend who he will be bringing to the event. Because the gentleman is—oh, how should I phrase this—somewhat of a public figure and not a member here but knows of your friend Samantha, Mr. Winfield suggested the four of you attend as mutual friends. Given the unique circumstances, it's the logical way to proceed."

"So, no sexual expectations?" Jewels asked point blank.

"For your friend, Samantha? No, absolutely not," he assured her. "She is attending exactly as who she is—one of your best friends, and nothing, absolutely nothing, more is expected of her."

"How can you be sure?"

"Jewels, please trust me on this one. She's cover only."

Why do I need cover? Jewels thought to herself. Listening hard, reading between the lines, trying to fill in what wasn't being said, she finally asked, "So, Todd suggested this?"

"Yes. He's been one of our most preferred clients for years, and it was at his request that we ask if you'd be willing to be his date and bring along Samantha to accompany his associate."

Jewels sat absolutely still, processing the information. *How the hell do they know who Sam is anyway?*

Her handler waited patiently.

Something didn't feel right, but she couldn't pinpoint it. *Money,* she reminded herself, *it never lies. Follow the money. It always leads to the truth.*

So, she confessed, "I'm no math wizard, but at the rates they're charging guests to attend the event, we're talking a couple hundred grand just to get the four of us through the front door. Plus, our normal fees on top?"

"Correct."

"So, to be clear, you're telling me our Mr. Winfield is willing to drop what's going to be close to a quarter mil on a little dinner date for four?"

"Correct."

"Beyond me," Jewels said, shaking her head.

"Not really, it's the president of the United States."

"And don't forget George Clooney," she added, intentionally lightening the conversation.

"How could I?" her handler assured her, again with a little grin.

He's gay, Jewels realized, answering, "Still, that's a lot of money for a date."

"To some, a fortune no doubt. To others, perhaps not so much." He paused, looking into her facial expressions, deciding if he needed to continue.

Jewels offered up her charming smile but remained silent, allowing things to continue unfolding.

"Everything is relevant," he finally said, deciding to continue. "Especially money, power, and even sex."

She nodded in agreement.

"In my humble opinion," he continued in his soothing fatherly voice, "perception is in the eye of the beholder. Without it, we'd be lost in a world we could never understand."

"One man's ceiling is another man's floor."

"Precisely."

"We each live in our own comfort zone. Is that it?"

"Yes," he said radiantly, as if she'd just gotten an A on some test. "You have such a wonderful sense of self about you. You've grown to know and trust yourself."

Right, she thought to herself, knowing, or at least believing, he had no idea what had happened between her and Todd. *I've been a basket case over this guy since I met him.*

"Being centered like you are, you have a unique ability to communicate intimately on all levels, intellectually, emotionally, spiritually, and physically."

"At times," she offered lamely.

"Don't belittle yourself. You are one of our top assets. Not only because of your radiant beauty and natural charm, but because of your unique talents."

Yeah, like losing control to a total stranger, her smile revealing nothing.

"To most, our fees would seem to be," he said, pausing again, "shall we say, astronomical. But it's all in the eye of the beholder."

"You're right," she agreed.

"And then again," he continued, "we don't have to, nor do we even try to, justify our fees. We allow our discreet few to do that for us."

Jewels nodded, knowing The Spa catered to the elite, but remained silent. The meet had turned into a reconnaissance mission, and when gathering information, she'd learned years ago, silence is golden.

"You are one of the best we've ever had," her handled continued. "You are absolutely charming, delightful to be around, well-educated, and one of the most intelligent women I've ever met. They're still using your PhD dissertation on political economics at universities across the country, and you wrote that nearly twenty years ago. Personally, I think you deserve a Nobel Prize for that work."

Again, another charming smile. *Just keep talking.*

"As I pointed out earlier, your self-confidence, your self-esteem, is effervescent. People are attracted to you. You're genuine, and perhaps most importantly, you fully grasp how powerful the need for human intimacy is on all levels."

"Without it, we'd cease to exist," she added politely.

"Quite possibly," he said, nodding in agreement, thinking about what she'd just said.

She continued waiting patiently.

"Jewels, you're not afraid of intimacy while on assignment. Few—and please believe me when I tell you this—few, very few, can do what you do."

Jewels thought long before speaking. "I appreciate the opportunities you've given me over the years."

Her handler nodded, now giving her time to continue.

While listening to him, she'd decided not to mention anything about retiring. *Something's up*, her instincts told her, *and this is not the time.* Effortlessly shifting gears, she asked, "With the president being at the dinner, won't everyone attending have to have been cleared through federal security prior to even being approved for an invitation?"

"Of course, and that's one of the reasons Todd suggested your screenwriter friend."

Again, Jewels nodded, still wondering how they knew so much about her personal life outside the job.

"She's a bit of an icon herself these days," her handler continued, "in the industry, as they say, and given Clooney is hosting, she'll be a perfect fit."

Jewels couldn't help herself and asked, "Who exactly is this Mr. Todd?"

"Like I mentioned earlier, he's one of our clients."

"With what is obviously access into people's private lives?"

"Oh, Jewels, come now. Samantha has been one of your best friends for years, and with the success she's having right now, her previous Oscars and being nominated again this year, she's created her own publicity. It's not a stretch to think she'd enjoy attending the event."

"Of course she would," Jewels rebutted, "but you didn't answer my question. How did Todd know we were friends?"

"I honestly can't answer that question. I can tell you he didn't get any info from us."

Interesting, Jewels thought.

"But I'm confident he'd be glad to tell you if you ask him personally."

Jewels paused again, giving herself time. So much about this assignment was already off the grid, she needed time to process. Staying totally composed, shifting gears once again, she smiled and said, "I think Todd's absolutely right. Samantha would fill out our foursome nicely. Plus, who in their right mind wouldn't want to meet Clooney, right?"

"Splendid," her handler smiled. "If you'll be so kind as to extend her a formal invitation and then let me know if she's receptive, we can get all the necessary paperwork handled."

"Trust me, she's in, but she'll want to know who I'm setting her up with."

"Oh, Ms. Jewels, it's nothing like that. Not even a date. One of Mr. Windham's associates is a huge—how can I say this tactfully—a huge, Clooney fan. From what I hear, he practically begged Mr. Windham to put this evening together."

"He's gay?" she asked, guessing from her handler's inflections.

"You are a very perceptive woman," he said, smiling.

"Interesting."

"How so?"

"Things are actually starting to make sense now," Jewels offered, not wanting to set off any alarms. "I guess I was reading too much into things."

"So, you think she'll agree?"

"Are you kidding me? She loves Clooney . . . we both do."

"Splendid. Simply splendid," her handler said. "We'll get started on the personal clearances. I'll get you logistics with assignment details, security, and confirmation codes."

All standard operational procedure. "Thank you," Jewels said, thinking the conversation was over as she started to get up.

"Given the unique circumstances in that we're dealing with the president of the free world," her handler added, "we will be altering procedure just a little, requesting that you code in to confirm once you are all at the party."

Jewel's survival instincts fired off alarms again, but she immediately smiled to cover any signs of concern. "Certainly," she said casually, "understood. Whatever you need."

"Splendid." He paused. "Was there something else you wanted to discuss?"

Shaking her head, Jewels smiled. "No. I was apprehensive about Sam being involved."

"Totally understandable, dear," her handler told her. "Don't ever hesitate to contact me if you ever have any concerns. That's one of the reasons I'm here."

"Thank you," Jewels told him as he walked her to the elevator, which opened as soon they stepped in front of it.

"You all should have a wonderful evening," he added with a telltale smile. "Wish I was going myself."

I live with one, and yet I'll never understand gay men, Jewels thought to herself as the elevator doors closed.

Chapter 8

After talking with Fields, Steel decided to pull two of his officers off drugs and put them on Grey Suit. Utilizing his young detectives, Lisa Laughlin and Casey Hale, their assignment was to cruise the waterfront restaurants looking for behavior patterns. Alternating between working as a couple and then as singles, they were thoroughly covering the waterfront. The third task member of the Grey Suit operation Steel pulled from behind a desk. The oldest detective in the unit, Big Bill Franklin was going to be Steel's live bait once the kids got a handle on the operation, which wasn't proving to be as easy as everyone initially anticipated.

"Neither of us has seen Grey Suit or Blazer since we started looking," Laughlin told her boss.

"Not a glimpse?" Steel wanted to know.

"Nada." Hale confirmed.

"What about any of the girls?"

"Surprisingly, no."

"No hook-ups at all," Laughlin added.

"I thought they'd made us during lunch, but I didn't think they'd be playing it this close to the vest," Steel offered. "If the girls aren't working, no one is making any bank, which means no one is going to be happy."

"Think they may have just moved their ops out of town for a while? Maybe down to Laguna or Dana?"

"Possibly," Steel agreed. "Tomorrow, head south and spend some time there. See if anyone shows."

"Boss, we haven't seen anyone we've recognized, but what if Grey has a larger stable than we initially gave her credit for. What if she's rotating girls?"

"Wouldn't surprise me, given you guys haven't observed anything remotely close to what you were seeing on a regular basis while on the drug bust."

"That's why I'm thinking; they've shifted locations."

"Alright, cover Laguna for forty-eight hours. See if anyone shows, and we'll take it from there," Steel summarized.

***

It had been a full week since Grey Suit had given the order to shut everything down, and the natives were getting restless, though not so much her girls. They didn't question Grey's orders. They had taken the week off, like from any normal job, some even going on vacation. A few of the girls had headed to Vegas, working the resorts on their own time, independently, which was allowed, making good money. But while they were working Vegas, they were on their own, no protection, no security, and if they got pinched, no legal team was behind them. Some of the younger girls thought the money they could earn on their own was worth it; the veterans knew better.

But Grey's problem wasn't with her girls; it was with her regulars. They were the one's complaining the loudest. *They just can't keep their dicks in their pants,* she thought to herself, sitting with Blue, looking out over the morning's still waters of the bay. She knew if she didn't start providing services again, soon, they'd move on, and what she'd painstakingly worked so hard to build would start to unravel. Her base clientele had taken years to establish, providing top-notch girls at reasonable rates in very secure environments. Word of mouth had slowly spread to where she was now running a couple dozen girls full time. She'd solidified key relationships within the establishments she based their operations from and had a half dozen charter yachts that were now fully dialed in on the operation. Everyone was earning, and it was all cash. Life was good, but she couldn't shake the feeling the heat had focused their beady little eyes in her direction.

"For whatever reason," she confessed, sipping her hot green tea, "I think the cops are looking at us."

"All because of that day at Billy's?" Blue asked.

"Yeah," she said, shaking her head. "There was something about that group that wasn't right. I don't know," she continued more to herself than addressing Blue, "maybe a mixed task force or whatever they call that shit when outside agencies work together." She paused, shaking her head. "Maybe I'm just being paranoid."

Blue knew better than to say anything. He waited patiently, letting her voice her thoughts if she wished.

She quit talking.

A few minutes later, her phone vibrated again. She ignored it. Clients had been calling her all week, initially wanting to book appointments, those that had appointments wanting to know why theirs had been cancelled, wanting to book new ones, and after being put off for a week, getting pissed nothing was happening. Grey knew she was going to have to do something.

Her phone vibrated again. Looking down reluctantly, she knew she'd have to answer this one.

"Hello, Trent."

"Paige, what the fuck!" Trent blasted, forcing her to pull the phone away from her ear.

"And a good morning to you too, sir."

"Quit the bullshit," Trent snapped. He was pissed and had every right to be; she'd been ignoring his calls the past couple of days. She knew she shouldn't have been, but she just hadn't been ready to deal with him, even though he was her number one man on the front lines.

He continued, "Paige, I'm fucking serious. This is bullshit. You, not taking my calls. We're running a fucking business here, and you run off and bury your head in the goddamn sand."

"Trent, I'm sorry. I really am," she offered lamely. "There's no excuse for leaving you hanging. I'm really sorry."

There was a brief pause from the other end.

"It won't happen again," she continued. "I promise."

There was another short pause. "Fucking-a," Trent said, calming down a notch. "This isn't like you, Paige. You're never off the grid, ever."

"I know, and Trent, again, I'm sorry."

"Well, what the fuck is going on? It's been over a week, and I haven't been able to tell anyone anything."

"I know," Paige told him. "I wanted to play it safe."

"I can understand that, and I appreciate it, but ducking and covering isn't going to solve anything."

"I know," she agreed with him. "You're right. Absolutely right. Like I said, it won't happen again."

"What's got you so spooked?"

She hesitated. Shutting down a multi-million-dollar cash business on women's intuition isn't a reason many men would understand, and Trent certainly wasn't one of them. So, she lied. "The Feds."

"What do you mean the Feds?" Trent screamed, forcing her to move the phone away from her ear for the second time.

"Please, quit yelling," she said after making him wait several beats.

"What do you mean the Feds?"

She lied, having no proof other than her gut feelings. "I pulled the plug last week because we're under surveillance by some joint task force."

"What the fuck are you talking about? What task force?"

"How should I know?" she snapped back. "But I do know the locals are working with the Feds, and they have us in their crosshairs."

"Holy shit," Trent mumbled. "No wonder you've been playing it close."

"Thank you," she said sarcastically.

"But why us?"

"How should I know?" Paige said. This entire week she'd had all ears to the ground, and no one had come up with anything. "No one knows anything," she added.

"This is the first I've heard about it, and God knows I'm usually on this shit before it even starts to stink."

"I know you are, and that's a big reason why I'm so worried." *Just keep blowing smoke up his ass,* she thought to herself.

"Damn, Paige. I'm sorry I yelled at you."

"I deserved it." *Time to add a little humble pie.*

"Not under these circumstances."

And top it off with some whip cream. "Don't worry about it," she said. "I should have let you know. I just didn't have any solid information and didn't want to concern you with some lame feeling I had about the whole thing."

"What do you think we should do?"

And I've got him. "Honestly, I'm not sure." She paused. "It's frustrating not knowing, not having a shred of information. And you haven't heard a thing?"

"Not a word."

"Nothing."

The conversation paused as both veterans of the trade pondered their situation. They'd worked together for years, respected, and for the most part trusted, one another. They were the talented core of a very-smooth-running, highly profitable, illegal operation that up until now had had virtually no problems with the law. They knew the unwritten rules and stayed well within the boundaries.

"It's a strange deal," Paige finally offered.

"Yeah, I'd say so. Why the fuck are the Feds involved?"

"That's the question I've been asking myself all week," Paige confessed. "I just can't figure it out. We're not running an international operation here—no underage girls, no solicitations, no drugs, nothing. It doesn't make any sense. I just don't get it."

"Me either. What do you suggest?"

"I know you've been taking a lot of heat, and thank you for handling it. I know those guys can get really pushy when they're not getting their cookies."

"You're not kidding. Talk about fucking addicts. I swear to God, some of these assholes act as if they own the fucking girls, for Christ's sake."

"Well, most of them could if they wanted to."

"No shit," Trent confirmed. "It's only been a week and they're jonesing as if it's the end of the world."

"I'm thinking maybe just a few of our regs, get them set up, run a trip or two, and see what happens."

"You sure?"

"No, not at all, but I don't know what else to do. Like you said, they're addicts. If they're not getting their fix from us, they're going to get it somewhere else."

"Give the girls a heads-up that we think we're being watched a little closer than normal. Don't spook 'em, but remind them to handle themselves exactly as designed," Trent commanded. "Nothing, and I mean nothing, out of the ordinary."

"Will do."

"And assure them we've got their backs if anything does come down."

"When do you want to run the tests?"

"Whenever you're ready."

"Okay, I'll let you know."

"Thanks, Trent." Paige paused, half wanting to say how much she appreciated everything he did from his side but didn't.

"No worries," was all he said, disconnecting the call.

So, we're back in business, Blue thought to himself. *This could get interesting.*

***

"You ready to meet Clooney?" Jewels asked Samantha as soon as they were seated on one of the outdoor benches lining the boardwalk along Laguna's main beach. They'd parked behind the liquor store after ordering a couple of Acai bowls from the Orange Inn before walking the half block to the beach.

"I couldn't believe it when you called and told me," Samantha answered. "I was actually introduced to him once at one of the post parties."

"You never told me."

"It was for like a second. He smiled. I melted. Said nice to meet you and was gone. He wouldn't remember me if his life depended upon it."

"But still, you got to meet him."

"Yeah, and he's ten times more handsome in person."

"I can't wait," Jewels confessed. "This is going to be so much fun."

"It should be," Samantha said, "but I've got to ask, what's going on? Jewels, are you alright?"

"I'm fine," she said, pausing, "but I'm afraid I have a crush on this guy. Or at least I haven't been able to stop thinking about him since we met."

"I love it. My hardcore professional falling for a john."

"You're so mean."

"I love it. Seeing you actually experiencing some feelings for a man."

"I hate it."

"Only because you hate not being in control. That's what scares you."

"Damn right. I hate feeling vulnerable."

"Welcome to the real world."

The women looked at one another and smiled.

"It's about time, is all I can say." Sam added, "Enjoy the ride."

"So far it sucks."

"So, for this Clooney gig, are you recruiting me?"

"Are you kidding me? Hell no. There's no way."

"Now I'm hurt."

"Don't be a goofball. This is nothing more than a good old-fashioned double date."

"Yeah, right."

Jewels went on explaining what she'd discussed with her handler about the evening, right down to the paperwork. "How's that for details?"

"Good, except for one thing."

"What's that?" Jewels asked innocently.

"How much?"

"How much what?"

"Come on, girl. Don't play coy with me. How much are you making?"

Jewels let out a long sigh, meeting her friend's eyes. "Ten grand."

"Are you kidding me?"

Jewels shook her head. "No. Standard fee."

"I want in," Sam demanded.

The girls got up and started walking south along the boardwalk past the lifeguard tower.

"So, we're all cleared," Sam asked.

"One hundred percent."

"I can hardly wait," Samantha said, thinking out loud. "We're going to need to go shopping."

The girls were almost the identical size. "If we're going on assignment together, I don't see any reason I can't get you cleared for a guest pass into my secret closet."

"Sounds good. How does your morning look?"

"Wide open."

"Then it's a date."

"My place around ten?"

"Perfect," Sam said. "Now, details please, starting at the very beginning."

Jewels did as was requested, starting from how she was initially recruited and continuing on, covering highlights of her illustrious career.

"I'm loving this," Samantha said, encouraging her to continue. "I had no idea."

"And we haven't even begun to scratch the surface," Jewels added.

Samantha was shaking her head. "All this time and I had no idea. So, tell me about our upcoming evening dancing with the stars," she asked excitedly. "Tell me more about Mr. Wonderful."

"I think you'll like him. Very handsome, polite and, ah, well, he's . . ."

"What?"

"Extremely talented."

"Oh, do tell."

Jewels paused, thinking about how to phrase it. "Skills the likes of which pretty much blew me away?"

"Seriously?"

"Dead serious. In fact, he's the one that got me thinking about getting out."

"How come?"

"Not sure exactly," Jewels confessed honestly. "Normally, unless the guy is into some submissive thing or some weird shit and I'm actually role-playing with him, for the most part assignments are just straight-up sex. I'm pretty much in total control. It's my job to make them think they're all badass studs, or whatever, rockin' my world and all, but basically I'm running the show the entire time." Jewels paused, again meeting Sam's eyes. "But with this guy, well, let's just say after twenty years as a professional, thinking I'd seen it all, he surprised me."

"That's saying something," Samantha said, nodding her head. "Was it anything specific? Some mystical technique or something?"

"No," Jewels told her, shaking her head. "Not really. It's hard to explain."

"I've certainly got nowhere more interesting to be," Sam urged her on.

"He had physical skills, no doubt. Some men have game, some good techniques, whatever, but he was different. He had a way about him that made me feel . . ." Jewels searched for the right word. "Safe."

Sam nodded, knowing exactly what Jewels was referring to. "A rare experience, to say the least."

"When I was with him, he made me feel as if nothing in the world could hurt me." She paused again. "Not just safe, but totally secure. He created a space . . . an energy around us. Like we were the center of the universe, in our own little cocoon, and nothing from the outside world mattered."

"Think maybe it was being on the yacht?"

"No," Jewels answered immediately. "I've had dozens of assignments on that boat. I love being onboard, but this had nothing to do with the boat. It was different. What he brought to our little party, what he created, was all-consuming."

"A unique individual for sure."

"No doubt. He made me want to be with him, no questions asked. I found myself craving his intimacy. I wanted him to want me . . . to trust me. In this business, that never happens."

"Hell, it hardly ever happens in real life."

"I know," Jewels answered, confirming what every woman has learned the hard way. "He made me feel not only wanted, but that he actually needed me. That I was more . . ."

Sam finished her sentence. "Than just a warm body?"

"In a sense, yes. That was part of it, but there was more than that. Creating intimacy between us was far more important to him than getting off."

"I can see how that would throw you."

"It did, especially at first. Normally, I'm the one who is offering up the 'girlfriend' experience, just enough intimacy and tenderness so they feel they're getting more than just sex. But this guy . . ." Jewels paused again. "Swept me off my feet."

Samantha nodded as Jewels continued.

"At first I was just curious, and then I actually became intrigued by his approach, but once he got rolling, I couldn't help myself from going with him and found myself totally surrendering to his touch, losing myself in the moment."

"Sounds awesome."

"Yeah, it was, being turned on like that by a total stranger." Jewels paused again, looking her friend in the eye before confessing the total truth. "I actually passed out."

"No you didn't."

"I did. Coming to, waking up in bliss, slowly regaining consciousness from some faraway place inside that's beyond description. I've never experienced anything like it or even close to it." Pausing. "Sam, I'd never felt that connected to another human being before in my life."

"Sounds like heaven."

"That's a good way to put it . . . like touching the hem of the garment."

The girls crossed Pacific Coast Highway and were now walking along Ocean Avenue past galleries, restaurants, and shops, but they just as easily could have been walking on the moon, in a world of their own, as Jewels continued.

"I'm afraid if I see him again, I may never be able to ever get enough of him."

Sam nodded with a little grin on her face.

"What are you smiling at?" Jewels asked.

"Sounds like my little call girl may really be falling in love."

"Sam, you know, that thought scares the bejesus out of me."

"He sounds fascinating."

"Like I said, I think you'll like him."

"He sounds intriguing."

"I honestly know virtually nothing about the man."

"Other than his sexual prowess," Samantha added with a sly smile.

"I'm telling you, it was way more than sexual."

Samantha nodded, then asked, "Okay, what about my official date? What do you know about him?"

116

"Other than he's a raving queen for Clooney, I have no idea."

"This could be one of the most interesting evenings I've had in a long time. Thanks for including me."

"It was actually Todd's idea," Jewels told her without really thinking.

Samantha frowned. "How does he know who I am?"

"That's the first question I'm going to ask him when I see him. I don't know. My handler—"

"Your handler?" Samantha asked.

"Yeah," Jewels paused, "that's what I call my contact. Pimp sounds so crude."

"Agreed."

"Get this. I've even created this entire fantasy about our upcoming assignment," Jewels confessed.

"Do tell," Sam urged.

"We work for a top-secret government agency as sexy undercover agents."

"Like Charlie's Angels."

"Our assignment at the fundraiser is to expose an offshore money laundering scheme to buy the presidency."

"And then what?"

"That's as far as I've gotten so far."

"Do we have guns strapped to the inside of our thighs?"

Jewels looked at her friend. "No," she countered, smiling. "Because we're wearing slinky evening gowns, and any concealed weapons would be easily visible through the sheer material."

"So, we're going in cold?"

"Yeah, with nothing more than our wits and our double-oh-seven iPhone guns."

"I can't wait."

***

"Laguna was a bust, Sarge," Detective Laughlin reported back at headquarters the next morning.

"Not surprised, they don't normally get much traffic down there anyway," Steel responded.

"But still worth a look-see," Detective Hale said.

"Agreed," Steel confirmed.

"What about Dana?" Laughlin asked. "From what we've seen thus far, it looks as if their operations are based along waterfront locations. Dana's got a pretty substantial set of marinas and high-end restaurants; it could be prime real estate."

"That's true, Detective, but they don't have much of a harbor, just that channel inside the jetty. So, running bay cruises like they do up here would be way too easy to spot," Steel summarized.

"Good point. I can't see them running outside, clients getting seasick and all. They could have moved up to Huntington, but those waters are pretty skinny as well."

"Same with Oceanside, which leaves Long Beach and San Diego."

"Both way out of our jurisdiction."

"So, what's next, Sarge?"

"Let's give the spots up here another look. It's been a week; that's a long time without any cash exchanging hands."

***

Late the next morning, Detectives Laughlin and Hale were seated together in the small intimate outdoor patio at Billy's when the first strawberries they'd seen in over a week showed up and sat down directly in front of them at the little Tiki bar. Both the girls were attractive, mid-twenties. Dressed suggestively in short skirts and tight halter tops, they weren't so out of the ordinary to actually scream working girls, but just enough so that if someone was looking they wouldn't need to second guess themselves. The detectives kept their conversation quiet and to themselves, observing the interaction between the bartender and the girls.

After a few minutes, Hale whispered to his partner, "I get the feeling he's in on this."

"Looks like, but hard to tell for sure," Laughlin countered. "Could be nothing more than typical bartender banter. Those girls are cute, and he could just be flirting with them. There's no one else at the bar, but worth keeping in mind."

No sooner than she'd said that than two older gentlemen in their mid-fifties came strolling into the patio and directly up to the girls. They all greeted one another by name, like old friends. There were hugs all around before taking seats, the guys bookending the girls between them.

The detectives managed to snap off a few quick images with their iPhones held subtly just off the table while the greetings were taking place. The gentlemen ordered drinks—cheers all around when they arrived—and they settled into somewhat relaxed conversation the detectives couldn't hear. To the casual observer, nothing more than just drinks with friends.

About twenty minutes later, a second round of drinks and the group got up, drinks still in hand, and headed towards the outdoor exit on the patio that opens directly to the marina in front of the restaurant.

"Did you see anyone pay the bill?" Laughlin asked as the group continued down the ramp towards the yachts.

"No."

"Interesting. Gives credence to the bartender being in on the deal."

"Hard to imagine there not being some connection."

"Agreed," Laughlin said as they continued watching the foursome board one of the dozens of beautiful yachts all perfectly maintained and docked inside the marina. The group was greeted by the boat's captain, dressed in whites. They didn't observe any deckhands or other crew members as the captain untied the lines himself, jumped back onboard, and skillfully backed a beautiful sixty-foot Viking out of its slip and into the bay. The detectives watched as the boat turned and began heading away from the restaurant at idle speed.

"You know, with the size of this harbor, at that speed, they could cruise inside the bay for a couple hours and never go past the same place twice."

"Makes for a pretty good set-up."

"Safe, secure, just one more boat taking a leisurely cruise around the bay."

"Plus, they could see any heat coming from miles away. If anything was going on below decks, everyone could be dressed by the time they were boarded."

"I'd say better than good; that's about as smooth an operation as it gets."

"You know we're just speculating," Laughlin added.

"Yeah, right. And those old men were just taking their nieces out for an afternoon of sightseeing."

***

Steel listened as his detectives reported back, nodding in agreement with their assessments. "Any sign of Grey?"

"No."

"Looks like they've got this thing down to a science."

"Very clean. We didn't see an exchange of money. In fact, they all seemed to have known each other for some time."

"Regulars maybe." Steel said.

"Makes sense, given how casual and friendly everyone was."

"Very buttoned up. Polished and professional. No tells. Going to be hard nailing them for solicitation."

"You're right."

"Let's see if we can figure out how they're generating new clients."

"Assuming it's word of mouth, no way they're reaching outside their inner circle."

"No shortage of bored, wealthy, cheating husbands around here."

"Let's see if we can figure out how they're recruiting new girls."

"My guess, same thing. The money's so good, the girls bring in their friends—spread the wealth, a nice, neat, tight little family."

"From the looks of things, neither approach is going to be easy," Laughlin offered. "Any suggestions, Sarge?"

"Bill is standing by, but I'm wondering if you think it would be easier getting inside as a new girl?"

"Honestly, boss, from what we've seen, my gut tells me Grey handpicks every one of her girls; it would be a long shot."

"You're probably right, but let's not rule it out. Their business exists because of strange, so you know they have to always be bringing in fresh girls."

"Like you said, my money is on the girls themselves bringing in their friends."

Everyone nodded in agreement.

"You know the money is good. It's not a hard sell to convince one or two of your friends, telling them they will make more in a couple hours than what they make in a month serving cocktails, working behind a counter somewhere, or slinging hash."

"By going down on some old fat fart? No way, not for me."

"Not for everyone, that's for damn sure."

"It always comes down to the money, how far is someone willing to go to get it."

"True," Steel confirmed. "For now, check with the Sheriff's Department down at the Harbor Patrol office and see if they've noticed anything unusual, any particular boats that seem to be cruising the harbor more than usual."

"Boss, they're all about safety and rescue down there. Not a lot of detective work happening on the water."

"I know, but if you ask really nice, flash 'em that seductive smile of yours, let 'em in on what we're looking into."

"Maybe."

"And make sure they know if anything comes down, we'll include them."

"Yeah, right. They're not going to buy that crap. They may drive boats, but they're not stupid."

"You're right. Fuck it," Steel admitted, "just ask about the boats."

"Yeah, they're going to love that too. Newport is one of the busiest harbors in the world, and we're going to waltz into their headquarters asking if they've noticed any particular boats cruising around more often than others."

"They're going to think we're the dipshits."

"You can count on it."

"Who knows, maybe one of 'em will at least think about it. Worth a shot."

"We'd be better off pilfering the webcam footage from the yacht clubs."

"You want to spend a thousand hours going over all that footage, be my guest."

"Just saying."

"Stupid idea."

***

Grey received a call from the bartender at Billy's as soon as the detectives left. "Yes, ma'am," he confirmed, "it was the same couple that's been in here over the past couple of months."

"Any glitches?" Grey asked.

"I saw them get off a couple low-angle shots when the guys arrived. Very subtle, but they were snapping for sure."

"Anything else?"

"No, ma'am. Standard procedure. Friendly greetings all around, like old friends, a couple of drinks and then down to the boat."

"What did the cops do when the boat left?"

"Hung around for another ten minutes and split."

"Okay, thanks, Tony. We have another group scheduled for this afternoon. Regulars, so we shouldn't have any issues, but let me know if the cops show back up."

"Absolutely, will do."

"Be on your toes."

"Always, ma'am."

***

As his detectives headed out to speak with the harbor master, Steel got on his cell to Fields.

"Looks like they're testing the waters," he told her, giving her a rundown of what he'd just discussed with his detectives.

"Hmm," Fields grunted. "Not much, but it looks like they want to get things back into gear."

"Any suggestions?" Steel asked her, knowing full well the depth and implications of that question, as did Fields.

Fields paused before answering, "What can I do to help?"

Steel smiled to himself, knowing they were on the same page. "You're already doing it," he said, making Fields smile, her day taking a turn for better.

Chapter 9

The Spa's command central received an unusual encrypted message the afternoon of the Clooney fundraiser, reading: Mission Critical. Jewels' handler decided not to put any extra pressure on her by passing this along to her as she and Samantha entered The Spa.

Having received clearance to accompany Jewels into the private lounge, Samantha stood at the doors of Jewels' walk-in and stared in awe. "Are you kidding me?"

Jewels smiled, "Nice, huh?"

"I'm blown away," Samantha said as she started fanning through the incredible wardrobe.

"I told you we didn't really need to go shopping, that I had us covered."

"Covered indeed," Samantha said, still in awe. "There's over a half a million in here."

"Easily," Jewels answered causally. "They require us to look nice and be prepared for any occasion at a moment's notice."

"And they pay for all this?"

"Yep."

"Fuck me," was all Samantha could utter.

"That's my job," Jewels said, smiling. "Pick something out," she added with a nonchalant wave of her hand. "Whatever you want. Everything should fit you perfectly."

The girls had been borrowing one another's clothes since college. Back in the day, borrowing outfits was out of desperation and necessity. Over the years, it had become a little ritual they both still liked doing, but Samantha had never seen this side of her friend's secret life.

"Where do I sign up?" Sam asked, thumbing through the ample selection of beautiful evening gowns. "I'm serious, I want in."

Thirty minutes later, the girls were dressed and ready for the red carpet. Needless to say, they both looked stunning.

"Ready?" Jewels asked, smiling, standing together in front of the full-length mirrors.

"Absolutely," Sam responded immediately.

Samantha didn't utter a word as they left the dressing lounge, entered the private elevators, and stepped into the limo. Settling into the plush back seat, Darryl met Jewels' eyes in the rearview mirror. "We're picking up the gentlemen at the Four Seasons."

Jewels' nod told her driver she already knew where they were heading. Looking over at her friend, she asked, "Nervous?"

Samantha shook her head. "Hell no. Excited, but not nervous."

"Good," Jewels assured her, "nothing to be nervous about. Tonight should be a lot of fun," she added, not having told Samantha any of the details about what her real assignment was for the night—or at least what she'd been led to believe was her real assignment. Jewels was the one trying to cover up her own nervousness. Inhaling through her nose, she forced herself to take some slow, deep, relaxing breaths.

Looking over at her, Samantha asked, "Are you alright?"

"I'm fine," Jewels lied, "just a little nervous about seeing Todd again."

***

Darryl called ahead, letting the valet service know they were arriving. Todd Windham and the other gentlemen were exiting the hotel's front doors as the limo pulled into the gently sweeping, wide, cobblestoned circular driveway of the beautiful Four Seasons. Pulling to the entrance, a white-gloved valet opened the door, and the gentlemen stepped inside the perfectly detailed chariot.

"Good evening, ladies," Todd said pleasantly. "Jewels," he said warmly, nodding as he looked into her eyes, "it's good seeing you again."

"Likewise, Todd," she replied, her breath catching in her throat.

"May I introduce you to a good friend of mine," Todd continued. "This is Jim Clark."

Jewels extended her hand as both gentlemen sat down in the seat facing backwards towards the ladies. "My pleasure."

"The pleasure is all mine," Jim assured her with a deep soothing voice.

"This is one of my best friends," Jewels said, continuing the introductions, "Samantha."

"I must say, you both look absolutely beautiful tonight," Jim continued in a gentlemanly, almost fatherly manner.

The ladies both nodded and smiled.

"You look familiar," Jim addressed Samantha before Jewels could complete the formal introductions.

"We had the pleasure of meeting briefly," Samantha told him, "at one of the premiers last year."

Jim paused, "That's right," he said excitedly, "you're the writer."

Samantha nodded.

"Sorry I didn't recognize you immediately," he apologized.

"Don't be," Samantha assured him, "we were only briefly introduced. No reason for you to have remembered me."

"Nonsense," he said. "I'm an idiot for not remembering you immediately. It's not every day someone has the good fortune of being introduced to greatness."

"Now you're being ridiculous," Sam told him.

"Not at all," Jim told her. "I love your work."

"Thank you," Sam said graciously.

"Now that we're having an opportunity to get reacquainted," he continued without meeting a beat and in typical Hollywood fashion, "may I request you ask your agent to let me have a chance at optioning your next project."

"I don't really have anything to do with that end of things," she said, looking him in the eyes. "I just write."

"Smart," he said, "very smart. Leave all that ugliness to someone else." Now looking at Todd, he said, "You didn't tell me we were going to accompany such beautiful, talented young ladies."

"Yes, Todd," Jewels chimed in, "what did you tell him about us?"

Todd smiled. "I could only speak for you," he said, looking Jewels in the eyes, "because until now I have not had the pleasure of meeting Samantha." They held one another's eyes. After a beat he continued, "James, why don't you tell the girls what I've told you."

"Only that you, Miss Jewels," Jim said, drawing her eyes away from Todd to meet his, "were one of, if not the most beautiful and charming woman he'd ever met." He paused, letting that sink in before continuing, "and that he could only imagine," shifting his gaze to Samantha, "that any friend of yours would be equally as charming."

The rest of the drive into the Hollywood hills was filled with chilled Dom, laughter, and easy conversation.

Arriving at the base of the hill to Clooney's house, they found themselves in the middle of what appeared to be the scene of a horrible accident. Dozens of police cruisers and unmarked black SUVs were everywhere, lights flashing in all directions. Adjacent streets leading to the scene were all blocked. Fully armed SWAT were everywhere. News vans were parked at all angles, their satellite dishes extended towards the heavens, beaming live feeds into the universe. Reporters with wireless handheld microphones jockeyed for position. Bathed in the bright key lights coming off the tops of the cameras of their respective shooters added drama to the scene. The reporters and their cameraman were all corralled inside a wide yellow tape barrier along the sides of the street that seemed to stretch endlessly in both directions, separating the media from the hard blockades that had been erected behind the media section, keeping the masses of onlookers back. Hundreds of photographers sent thousands of white-hot flashes into the limos as they inched past them, each limo holding VIPs and A-list stars. The paparazzi hoping for that one shot that might penetrate the dark-tinted windows and make the tabloids.

As the vehicles continued creeping forward, dark-suited men backed by SWAT teams approached each vehicle. Packets of official envelopes were handed out of the front window by the drivers. Individual federally issued ID cards retrieved from the packets were swiped by mobile scanners for authentication. Each vehicle was required to roll down their passenger's windows for visual verification of each occupant. This is when the photographers' flashes exploded, filling the night with blinding strobes of light. As their limo approached the front of the line, they saw that every vehicle was being swept down both sides, front to rear, with illuminated mirrors on telescoping arms, scanning the underside. The drivers were asked to exit the vehicles and open the trunks; bomb-sniffing dogs were working overtime.

"This is nuts," Jewels said.

"Never seen anything like this," added Jim, "not even for the Academy Awards. This is insane."

"The president's detail," Todd added calmly. "Standard procedure."

"Amazing," Samantha added. "Can't even imagine how much all this costs."

"You don't want to know," Todd told her, adding, "the price we pay since 911."

"Is it like this everywhere the president goes?" Jewels asked innocently.

"Pretty much," Todd told her. "This is worse than normal because of all the celebrities."

Jewels couldn't help herself, asking Todd, "How do you know so much about this?"

Todd looked her in the eyes again. "I don't. Not really," he said, hoping to brush her inquiry aside. "Nothing more than from watching ordeals like this on TV."

Jewels wasn't buying it. Her radar was up and pinging, but she decided to let it go. "Yeah, I guess," she said, lowering her eyes. "Pretty much standard procedure."

"Nothing more," Todd tried assuring her. "We'll be through this in a few minutes and on our way up the hill to what should be an incredible party."

"I'll drink to that," Samantha said, holding her champagne glass up for a toast. Everyone touched crystal and they were indeed on their way.

Police and government vehicles lined both sides of the street all the way up to Clooney's house. Police helicopters from above swept the surrounding homes and lush landscaping with bright lights and infrared cameras, and high above them more powerful technologies were also fully focused on the scene below.

Arriving at the entrance to Clooney's house, their individual IDs were once again rechecked and confirmed before being allowed onto the premises.

***

Fields was pissed she'd been assigned the detail. *This is all CIA bullshit*, she thought to herself as she scanned Jewels' ID card, comparing the recent photo to her face. *Beautiful*, she thought as she handed the ID back while instructing her to "Please put your handbag in the tray and step into the metal detector." *At least I'm up here playing TSA agent*, Fields tried to console herself, *instead of down the hill dealing with the mass of insanity.*

"Please step forward," she repeated on auto. "ID please." Looking up to Samantha's face, she thought, *Where do all these fucking drop-dead beautiful women come from?*

***

The entrance to Clooney's home was stunning. When most people think of Southern California, palm-lined streets and white-sand beaches come to mind, but the entry to Clooney's house was beyond words. Huge ferns, giant palms, and colorful flowers in full bloom were everywhere. The garden leading to the house was as lush as any tropical paradise in the world. Perfectly designed exterior lighting subtly illuminated the walkway while accenting the garden. A backlit cascading waterfall spilled over smooth river-rock boulders and into a deep pool that streamed directly under the walkway just before the entrance.

So, this is how the other half lives, Jewels thought to herself, looking at Samantha, who was reading her thoughts.

As they stepped inside a quiet outer foyer, several well-dressed men, the outlines of their weapons visible under their suits, greeted them with polite nods. A handsome young man wearing a perfectly tailored black tuxedo asked, "May I take your coats, ladies?"

Their photos had been taken while in the garden, and having already been facially matched to their IDs, there was no need for claim checks here. Every individual was confirmed and logged in, right down to who was wearing and carrying what as they entered the premises.

Hotel California, Jewels thought to herself as they entered the party. All the beautiful people knew they were finally in a secure place, out of camera shot, clear of the long lenses and prying drones of the media; time to let their hair down and party. To say the festivities were in full swing as they walked in was an understatement.

"Holy shit," Samantha had to virtually shout into Jewel's ear to be heard. "Can you believe this?"

Imagine what a private party hosted by one of the biggest stars on the planet might be like, times it by a million, and you might be close. The party was beyond imagination. Jewels was nowhere near prepared for what she found herself in the middle of. Lights, no cameras, and action ... they were instantly engulfed in a frenzy of swirling energy.

"This is insane," Jewels said, trying to take it all in at once. She'd been to some raging parties in her day, but nothing even came close to this. Perfectly sculptured, chiseled, handsome young men in only skintight, jet-black tuxedo pants, leaving nothing to the imagination, and white bow ties around their necks were everywhere, carrying silver trays with all sorts of drinks. Beautiful, topless young women wearing only the same black tuxedo pants and white bow ties as the men were offering guests trays covered with exotic foods. Live music was streaming in from outside in the huge, covered garden, which dwarfed the entry grounds by comparison. People were everywhere, dancing, mingling, laughing.

Their drink needs were instantly attended to. In the midst of all the chaos, somehow the extremely well-trained waiters and waitresses recognized new guests the second they arrived and were beside them in an instant with their offerings.

"Glad you came?" Todd asked Jewels.

Touching glasses, she leaned in, giving him a kiss on the cheek.

"Oh my God," James managed to get out. "There he is . . . there's Clooney. Catch me before I faint."

Samantha wrapped her arms around his shoulders. "No, you keep me up."

Jewels watched as Clooney and Todd made eye contact. Clooney immediately smiled and started towards them. *Holy shit*, Jewels realized, *they know each other. Fuck me* was all she could think to herself as the two men covered the short distance between them and gave one another a big hug.

"I swear to God I'm going to faint," James uttered before collapsing into the overstuffed chair next to him, Samantha collapsing with him, landing on his lap.

"George, I'd like to introduce you to my friend, Jewels," Todd said. "Jewels, George Clooney."

Jewels was speechless, staring into his eyes.

Taking her hand, "Pleasure to meet you," George said warmly, his eyes twinkling as his billion-dollar smile filled the room. He'd seen a reaction like hers a thousand times before. "Todd said you were a stunning creature, but there's no way he could have described how truly beautiful you are."

Jewels felt her legs buckling when pure fear shot through her as she realized she was about to pee. She'd never been star struck before and actually had to squat down and cross her legs to keep from doing so.

This sent Sam and James over the edge. Looking over at the two of them giggling like little kids, Todd added, "Obviously, big fans. George, may I introduce James and Samantha."

Being as cool as he is, George stepped around the squatting Jewels and actually sat down on top of both James and Sam. "Mind if I join you?" he asked, paraphrasing a Hollywood classic. "I'll have whatever they're having."

Todd held his hand out for Jewels, who immediately took it up but remained squatted. "You okay?"

She was speechless as good-spirited laughter filled the room.

***

And so the evening progressed, everyone having the time of their lives.

"I can't believe I almost peed my pants," Jewels confessed, shaking her head. "I feel like a schoolgirl."

"Now that's an idea," Todd added. "Pleated skirt, bobby socks, and a little white button-down blouse."

"You are a nasty man," Jewels rebutted, lowering her chin and batting her eyelashes. "Promise you won't spank me if I'm bad?"

"No way," he said playfully, "you know what happens when you're a bad girl."

Just then Jewels felt her phone vibrate. *Shit*, she thought to herself, *I forgot to check in after we got here.*

"I have to take this," she said.

Todd nodded. He understood as she stood up.

The message read: Connect Now.

Stepping away from Todd into a relatively quiet corner, she texted back: Awaiting Instructions.

The reply froze her in her tracks. Assignment: President of the United States.

Her world as she knew it suddenly came to an end.

Chapter 10

Todd hadn't taken his eyes off her since she'd stood up to check her message, but her body language instantly confirmed his instincts. The second she'd received the reply, he knew she'd been given her assignment. It was the moment the men he worked for had expended untold millions of dollars to make happen. Hundreds of hours in preparation and planning—the moment of truth. He felt his heart racing. He took several deep breaths, never taking his eyes off Jewels. *Patience,* he told himself, allowing his years of experience to take control. As much as he wanted to go to her, he forced himself to sit and wait for her to return. Her back was still to him. She hadn't twitched a muscle since reading the text.

Little did she know, parked just down the street, a dozen highly trained agents sat lined along the inside of a forty-foot trailer, glued to an entire wall of monitors. Every word of her encrypted text had been intercepted, recorded, and was now being decoded, as had every word and every move she'd made since leaving The Spa that evening been viewed in real time and recorded by another surveillance team far, far away.

***

Following strict protocol, in the months and weeks leading up to the fundraiser, Secret Service techs had installed a grand total of 176 hidden, 4K high-def wireless security cameras throughout and around Clooney's entire estate, gifting those watching from far away with more than they could have ever hoped for. They'd tried for years to get the target in range, but until now had never even come close. Now this. He was being handed to them on a silver platter. There wasn't a nook or cranny that didn't have live-feed, real-time audio and visual surveillance beaming into the van . . . and beyond.

The stage was set, the players in place. Now all the observers could do was to wait and watch what was about to unfold. All eyes focused on Jewels, both near and far.

<div style="text-align:center">***</div>

"The president," Jewels murmured to herself, her phone still up to her face, still trying to wrap her mind around this new assignment. *The president of the United States, they're out of their fucking minds. Think,* she told herself as the hairs on the back of her neck stood up.

Instinctively, she knew she was suddenly in treacherous waters. Nothing made any sense. The entire time she'd assumed her assignment was Todd, But now this. The couple of glasses of champagne she'd been nursing all evening had been enough to dull the machine-gun transmissions firing off out of control throughout her grey matter. A thousand questions were bombarding her at once. *Concentrate, goddamn it,* she told herself, *and figure out what the fuck is going on.* She forced herself to take a deep breath . . . then another. One fact became crystal clear. Todd set this up. *Had he just been scouting me on the yacht? Taking me for a test drive? Pimping for the President?*

"Fucking asshole," she said out loud.

"Is everything alright?"

She practically jumped out of her skin. "What?"

"Is everything alright?"

Looking up from her phone, a towering giant of a man had silently come up behind her and was now standing just inches away, asking if everything was alright.

She heard her voice ask again from a distance, without even realizing she was speaking, "What?"

"Are you alright?"

No, I'm not alright! "Who are you?" she managed to get out.

"Ma'am, the president would like to see you."

***

Fuck! Todd screamed to himself, instantly springing from his seat. He'd been so focused on Jewels that he'd failed to notice the behemoth of an agent approaching her from around the corner. He covered the short distance between them in a few powerful strides, but he was too late. "Jewels" was all he was able to get out before being cut off by three additional agents.

Hearing her name, she whipped her head around in time to see Todd being whisked away by several men dressed identically to the giant who was now leading her down a private, deserted hallway.

"Todd!" she cried out.

"Don't worry, ma'am," the giant whispered, his arm wrapped firmly around her waist with a grip she knew she couldn't escape.

"Don't ma'am me," she snapped defiantly. "Who the fuck are you?"

"The president only has a few minutes," the giant hissed in a low, commanding voice. "Shut up and do your job."

She sensed he wasn't all that thrilled about the task at hand but was in no way wavering. As the full impact of what was happening overwhelmed her, she felt her legs buckle. "No," she pleaded. "I don't want to do this."

"Ma'am, this is all on you, not me."

"No, it's not. I didn't agree to do this."

Stopping abruptly, he snapped her body around like a twig, glaring into her eyes, telling her in no uncertain terms, "Yes, you did. You do this for a living. So, shut up and do your job."

"Fuck you," she screamed, fighting to break free. Instantly, the mammoth's massive hand covered her mouth and nose as his other hand grabbed a fistful of her hair, jerking her head back.

Forcing her to meet his glaring stare. "You're going to step through that door and do what you do best, so quit acting like a little bitch and do your fucking job."

Shaking her head, she screamed, "No!" but not even a muffled sound came out from under his iron glad hand. They stared into one another's eyes. Suddenly, she realized she couldn't breathe.

Like a deer caught in the headlights of a speeding car, she stared at the giant in disbelief.

Forcing her to turn toward the door, it opened as if on command. The giant released her, half guiding, half shoving her through the door. It immediately closed behind her, leaving her alone in a dimly lit room. Moments later, before her eyes could fully adjust, she heard his unmistakable voice. She couldn't believe what was happening. The president of the United States was standing behind her, telling her what to do.

"Don't turn around," he commanded as she felt his hands reach around under her arms, grabbing both breasts through her sheer dress, squeezing his fingers, finding and pinching her nipples. His mouth was on the back of her neck, biting at her delicate skin, his breath reeking of booze. She felt his hardness pushing against her. Before she knew it, he had her bent over the arm of an overstuffed chair. His hands frantically pulling up her

138

dress, he grabbed her panties, pulling them down in one rapid motion. Wedging his knees between her legs, he forced them open.

"Fucking cunt," he hissed, forcing himself inside her in one powerful thrust, slapping her ass hard. "Take this, you no-good fucking whore," he growled.

***

"Cut the feed," screamed the agent in charge of the surveillance unit. A beat passed, and the monitor displaying Jewel's exposed white ass with the fully aroused president inside her was streaming in living color. "Now, goddammit!" screamed the AIC. "Cut the feed."

The monitor went black, but the wireless signal continuing to beam into the heavens wasn't missing a frame, available to anyone with the technology to detect, intercept, and transcode such things. Funny thing about wireless transmitters, their job is to transmit. By whom, when, where or how said transmissions are received, well, that's a different story altogether.

***

Without a moment's warning, she suddenly felt herself tumbling towards the floor, landing hard, practically knocking the breath out of her lungs. Feeling the president being jarred out of her as they hit, she rolled, trying to get as far away from him as she could. She hit something hard—the wall, a desk, she couldn't tell—but it wasn't going anywhere. She instinctively pulled her knees up into a ball, trying to protect herself. She had no idea what was happening and then couldn't believe what she was witnessing in the dim light. Todd was straddling over the president, lifting him off the floor with one hand, his thumb and forefingers a vice grip, squeezing the nerve centers at the back of the president's neck, causing him to black out just as he jammed his knee into the president's groin, knocking his breath out as be crumbled unconscious into a heap on the floor.

***

"Goddammit!" the AIC screamed in the truck. "Burn it, burn the entire thing! I don't want a single frame of that shit readable."

The tech agent who had the misfortune of having that room as part of his sector didn't know what to do.

"I said burn the fucking files!"

"But, Chief, you know that's against regs," the agent pleaded.

"Fuck the regs!" the AIC snapped back. "We got POTUS banging some chick, and I don't want a frame of that shit rendered. Understand? Not a fucking frame. I don't give a shit about the regs."

"But—"

"No fucking buts! Burn it now!"

"Yes, sir," the agent replied.

The rest of the techs in the unit sat motionless, their collective eyes glued to the monitors in front of them. No one dared to even glanced towards the room's monitor, which was now black. No one wanted any part of this.

"Those fucking assholes he has pimping whores for him ought to be shot," the AIG continued steaming behind the row of techs sitting in front of the banks of monitors.

***

It was over in less than a few seconds.

140

Bending over, Todd reached out for her. She was shaking uncontrollably and didn't know what to do. Their eyes met, but only for an instant. "We have to go," Todd said.

She nodded that she understood, but she didn't move.

"Jewels, please, get up. We have to go," he said as gently as he could, pulling her to her feet. She was shaking like a leaf. She heard him repeat, "We have to go," but she could hardly stand.

Reaching down, she tried to pull her panties up from around one of her ankles, but as she bent over, something warm streamed down the inside of her leg. Realizing it was the president's semen oozing out of her, she started to faint. Todd grabbed her, holding her steady. Helping her pull up her panties and get her dress down, he brushed her hair out of her face. Knowing she was in shock, it broke his heart when a thin smile crossed her lips.

"We have to go," he said again in a gentle voice, as if talking to a child. "Now."

***

The president's personal detail had all been handpicked by the president himself over the course of his previous term. He'd gone through more agents in those first four years than all the presidents before him combined. Dozens of excellent agents, all good men, all willing to give their lives protecting him had all been dismissed by the president, one after another, for reasons no one could understand, their careers forever tarnished. The presidential detail that had once been the most coveted position an agent could achieve, under this administration had become a vicious cancer within the ranks of the Secret Service. The president's men had evolved into an elitist group of individuals known now within the agency as the Untouchables.

***

"Motherfuckers!" the AIC cursed again, knowing the Untouchables had staged the entire evening. "Fundraiser, my ass," he continued screaming. "Goddamned waste of fucking time. All this," he said, gesturing towards the wall of monitors, "just so that fucking asshole could get his rocks off. I hate this fucking job." Knowing that over a hundred million dollars had just been pissed away, pushed him over the edge. "I can't take this shit anymore." Rubbing his eyes, he ordered, "Get me the director."

***

The AIC's rage had given Todd the few precious seconds he'd needed to subdue the president and lead Jewels out of the same hidden door he'd entered moments before.

***

"Chief, it's oh three forty back east."

"I know what fucking time it is! Wake his ass up. I don't give a shit anymore."

His team loved him, and the last thing they wanted was to see him gone. He'd been doing battle behind the scenes with the Untouchables since it had become painfully apparent what the president had created.

"Chief, I have the director on com one."

"This better be good," the director of the Secret Service snapped in a sleepy voice.

"I quit," was all the AIC said and hung up.

***

Thousands of miles away, another secure phone buzzed in the dark.

"We got him."

"Please confirm."

"We got him." Pause. "But there may be a complication."

After a long pause on the receiving end, "Fix it."

"Understood."

***

Agent Fields had remained on her post outside the front door since arriving early that evening. The last of the guests had checked in and been cleared hours ago. She was tired, cold, and getting more irritated with every passing minute. Babysitting the empty entrance to a star's private party wasn't exactly what she'd signed up for. Suddenly, without warning or any coms, the president's limo came screeching out from the underground garage, speeding past her, down the cobbled driveway and out the front gate. There had been absolutely nothing out of the norm, when all of a sudden, out of nowhere, there was a mad panic to get the president out of the residence and away. Fields, along with the other officers assigned to the front door, weapons drawn, rushed the party. Pushing open the closed interior front doors, they froze in their tracks. The party was still in full swing—not a sign of trouble. They'd expected the worst, but there was nothing—no screaming, no panic, no one running for cover, just the beautiful people basking in the sunshine of their delusions.

"What the fuck?" Fields muttered out loud to no one in particular as everyone's radios lit up.

"POTUS has left the building. Repeat, POTUS has left the building."

"No shit," she said.

Their radios continued chirping. "Status clear. Repeat, status clear."

"Thanks for the head-up," she muttered, wondering to herself, *What the fuck is going on?*

***

Stepping from the room, Todd and Jewels found themselves alone in the hallway, music and laughter floating in from the adjacent rooms. Continuing down the hall, she thought to herself, *My knight in shining armor.*

The realization that Todd had just risked his life to save her from death by a thousand cuts hadn't even begun to take shape in her mind. Everything was a blur.

***

The couple of minutes it had taken the entire ordeal to transpire had been all the time Todd needed to get his highest-level clearance confirmed by the Untouchables, allowing him to enter the room unaccompanied through the secret passage.

The fact he'd attacked the president instantly catapulted him to the top of the most wanted man in the free world, at least as far as the Untouchables were concerned.

***

Everything had happened so fast. She couldn't even begin to come to terms with . . . what? She thought to herself, *Getting raped by the president of the United States.*

"Hang in there," Todd whispered into her ear. "We're almost there."

Not knowing what was happening, she continued clinging to him, going wherever he led.

The president of the United States. Her instincts never failed her. She knew with every fiber of her being that this was bad. Very bad. A cold chill shot through her entire body as she realized that this was just the beginning.

Todd was on full alert. If the Untouchables had sounded the alarm, they were done for. No way they were getting out of that house alive, but as they came to the end of the hallway, there was no alarm, no panic. The party was still in full swing, as if nothing had happened. He scanned the room, immediately spotting several Secret Service agents, earphones in place yet not doing anything. *Okay,* he thought to himself, *they're keeping a lid on it. We just might make it out of here alive.*

"Let's find Sam and James and get out of here. How does that sound?" No answer. He continued gently guiding her through the party. He spotted Samantha the same instant Jewels saw them.

"Don't say anything to them," she pleaded without looking up.

"Not a word."

"Hey, guys," James slurred from behind the umbrella of a tequila sunrise. "Can I buy you a drink?" laughing at his cleverness. "They're free," he added, toasting the air at his own joke.

Samantha sensed something was askew, seeing Jewels clinging to Todd. *Not her style,* she thought to herself, *something's wrong.* When Jewels didn't meet her gaze, any doubt was erased.

"What do you say we head for hills?" Todd offered, trying to keep things light.

Totally blitzed, James rebutted, "The party is just getting started. I don't want to leave, at least not until I get a goodnight kiss from our host."

"You couldn't handle a kiss like that," Samantha jumped in, sensing it was time to leave. "Trust me, James, you'd lose it."

145

"You're right. You're absolutely right, my love. I'd have a fucking heart attack and die on the spot, but what a way to go."

"How about we get out to the car, and I'll tell you all about my new book."

***

Instantly switching from pilfering the FBI's feed the moment it was cut to that of their own satellite, the Elites continued monitoring the scene below from far away. They had nothing from inside the residence, but when the foursome emerged out the front door, they had them again.

"Be sure we're grabbing all those news feeds."

"Recording every uplink, sir."

***

Once outside, they found themselves in the middle of the media blitz. Jewels buried her head inside Todd's jacket and whispered, "Please get me out of here."

Standing just ahead of them, Todd recognized Agent Fields from when they arrived. He tapped her on her shoulder. Reaching inside his coat pocket, he flashed her his credentials.

Fields recognized his status immediately, even though she'd always believed no such position, or person, really existed.

"We need out," Todd said, "now."

"My car is right over here," Fields said without hesitation, nodding towards her government-issued black Taurus parked parallel with Clooney's estate entrance.

"Let's go," Todd said, commanding the entourage.

No one hesitated, at least until they went to get into the car. Once the president had left, they'd opened the flood gates to the news cameras and paparazzi, who had recorded every frame of their departure from the party to the car.

"Where's our limo?" James inquired in his drunken stupor.

"This nice lady is going to give us a ride to the limo," Samantha assured him without missing a beat.

"Okay doe-kay," James said happily, falling into the back seat.

Samantha, looking to Jewels for an explanation but accepting things with nothing more than a nod from her best friend, climbed in next to James.

Todd held the door for Jewels, but she refused, squeezing his arm even tighter.

They walked together around to the passenger side front door and got in.

Fields looked at Todd for instructions, asking without having to say it, "Light it up?" Shaking his head no, Todd indicated with a nod towards the street. "Just get us out nice and easy."

But that proved to be easier said than done.

Trying to get any footage they could, every news producer on scene was frantically calling their stations, snapping off and sending images, then holding for any facial identifications they could get on the mysterious foursome. Finally, Samantha was identified and immediately became the focal point of the live feed.

"In a bizarre twist to the night, Academy Award winning writer/producer Samantha Graves was whisked away from the party in what appeared to be an unmarked Secret Service vehicle. Ms. Graves was accompanied by two unidentified men and a young woman."

***

With the president now off premises, the Secret Service and FBI were pulling out, leaving local law enforcement to deal with what had become a complete cluster fuck of converging limos and news vans. Gridlocked in a bottleneck on, in, and around Clooney's driveway, the limos jockeyed for position in a vain attempt to retrieve their sacred cargos. The news vans had simply stopped in the middle of the street after getting as close to the party as possible, raised their dishes to the heavens, and started filming anything that moved. As more and more paparazzi continued arriving, the party caught a second wind as the well-lubricated guests, especially those not prone to missing an opportunity of having their faces seen by the millions, started retrieving champagne and libations out of the logjammed limos. Playfully popping corks at the photographers, and with one of the limo's ample sound systems cranked to its max, some eventually got around to climbing out of the sunroofs and dancing on top of their sleek black chariots.

"They're dancing in the streets," chirped one of the perky young entertainment reporters, "or should I say, on top of the world. Live on the scene." Ecstatic at having made it to the curb in front of Clooney's estate. "Now this is what I'm talking about. Hollywood!" Her cameraman panning off her glued-on smile in time to capture a wasted Bieber dancing on top of a limo, doing his best impression of Kevin Bacon in *Footloose,* sliding down the windshield, across the spotless polished hood of the limo, before stumbling into the street, but keeping his feet and drawing a hardy round of applause from the crowd.

***

Stuck in the madness, Todd finally said, "This is bullshit. Light 'em up. Get us the hell out of here."

Flashing dark-blue and neon-white lights immediately illuminated from under the front grill and rear window, an ear-piercing screech, followed by the more traditional emergency siren, overpowering the ambient music, put a temporary end to the street party. Which was all they needed. The street parted like the Red Sea, limos squeezing out of their way, news vans frantically backing up over curbs, into shrubs, and onto neighboring lawns. A few minutes later, they were safely off the hill.

"Right on Sunset," Todd instructed. Fields obeyed without question.

The mood inside the car was somber. James had passed out the minute his butt hit the back seat, and Samantha and Jewels had yet to make eye contact. Todd and Samantha had exchanged glances but no words. Eventually, Jewels climbed over the back of the front seat and into Samantha's arms. She pulled her close, gently caressing her hair; it was a matter of moments before she felt the warmth of Jewels' silent tears on her chest. Looking up at Todd with inquiring eyes, Todd just shrugged his shoulders, eyebrows raised, shaking his head. *This is not good,* Sam thought, *not good at all.*

***

Initially, Fields assumed they were heading to headquarters, but as they neared the 405 and Todd hadn't said a word, she finally asked, "Where to?"

They were on a winding stretch of Sunset above the sprawling UCLA campus with exclusive, gated, private residential neighborhoods to their north.

"Pull in there," Todd said, pointing to a darkened campus parking lot.

Fields immediately went on full alert.

"This is good," he said.

They were alone in the virtually empty, dimly lit parking lot as she pulled to a stop.

This was the first time she'd really had an opportunity to look at him since he'd flashed her his credentials. Their eyes met, two seasoned professionals summing up the situation in a heartbeat. Fields didn't like being put in this position.

Todd saw her flinch. "It's okay," he said softly, trying to assure her. "Would you mind stepping outside with me for a minute so we can talk?"

Fields hesitated. Todd held out both hands, and with his left, reached inside his jacket, pulled out his gun and set it on the seat between them.

Fields didn't take her eyes off him, nor her right hand off her firearm.

"I just need to talk to you for a minute. Please, in private."

"Bullshit!" Jewels hissed. "If you've got something to say, I want to hear it."

"Jewels, please," Todd said, "there's some things I need to find out from the agent here."

After her little cry, Jewels had regained a little of her composure and was now getting pissed at him for even thinking of excluding her.

"I don't think so," was all she said.

The three women waited in silence for him to respond, each in her own way instinctively knowing what he did next would determine all of their futures.

"Okay," he said after letting out a long, deep breath.

***

In making the decision to pull Jewels out, Todd had put an end to his career and most likely his life. Pulling Jewels out from under that asshole of the free world, then jamming his testicles halfway up the guy's guts with his knee, had pretty much sealed the deal. Trying to come up with a plan before saying anything to the women, he found himself smiling at the sheer futility of it all, but none of it mattered anymore. He'd acted on total instinct, saving the woman he'd fallen in love with.

None of the women had taken their eyes off him since they'd stopped. Jewels finally broke the silence. "What are you sitting there smiling about?"

Todd looked her in the eye, then made eye contact with Samantha and Fields as well before speaking. "My grandfather told me the best way to make God laugh was to tell him your plan."

"What the hell are you talking about?" Samantha blurted out. "This is insane, and you're talking like you belong on the short bus instead of giving us orders from the front seat of a . . ." Looking around, Samantha realized she didn't have a clue. "Some secret Batmobile."

That broke the tension.

"Really, Sam?" Jewels inquired. "A Batmobile."

On cue, Fields pivoted around, extending her hand to the back seat, formerly introducing herself. Then, facing Todd, she asked point blank, "And you are?"

***

Onboard Air Force One, things weren't progressing quite so pleasantly. When he came to, a completely baffled president was clueless as to why he was curled up in pain, his groin packed in ice. His balls hurt so much he was afraid to even look at them.

"What the fuck happened?" he screamed, demanding answers no one could provide. Because no one knew. Some top-clearance Security Council asshole had pulled rank and, in a matter of seconds, had taken POTUS down. The Untouchables were scrambling to cover their own asses, because every man in the unit knew heads were going to roll.

***

Things weren't going much better at FBI headquarters. With the video feed being burned, then shut down for those precious few minutes, all they had to go on were the before and after videos showing nothing but an empty room. Phones were blowing up, and the director was going out of his mind. "How the fuck could something like this have happened!" he kept screaming over and over to no one in particular.

***

However, in faraway places, there was no confusion or any doubt as to what had happened. Every frame had been transmitted and recorded in 4K, with dual channel audio to boot. They had the president of the United States on tape having sex with one of their assets. Mission accomplished. But the reason why their assets had run off was unknown and unacceptable. Without having DNA, proof positive, in their possession, things could still go sideways. It was a very expensive lesson learned courtesy of a semen-stained blue dress that proved not to be enough evidence—not when dealing with the most powerful men in the free world.

***

Sitting in the darkened vehicle with the three women, Todd decided to come clean. He had nothing left to hide and, in all honesty, nowhere else to turn. When he'd intervened, he'd betrayed the trust that had taken him his entire career to build, the trust that fierce, ruthless enemies had both bestowed on him. The bridge from which they'd escaped was burning from both sides, and they were stuck in the middle. There was no going back.

"My name is Todd Windham. I'm a double agent working undercover for the NSA."

Fields stared at him, her hand resting on her gun.

"I'm sorry I got you involved with this," he said looking directly at Fields, "but the bottom line is there's no going back ... not for any of us."

Fields' training told her to secure his firearm, which was still sitting on the front seat between them, but her instincts were screaming at her to not move, to listen.

Reading her mind, seeing her conflict while knowing exactly what her training was, Todd slowly reached out with his left hand, picked up the firearm by its barrel, and offered it to her butt first.

On gut instinct alone, she refused it, her eyes never leaving his, saying instead, "You might want to hang onto that. From what you're saying, you may be needing it."

Todd felt a wave of relief wash over him as his right hand, hidden low and just behind his hip, released the trigger of his backup piece. It had been pointed directly at Fields' heart. His right hand came out from under his jacket and, taking the gun from his left hand, placed it back in his shoulder holster.

Never knowing how close she'd actually come to dying, Fields asked, "What now?"

"We don't have much time," Todd offered lamely. "It's not going to take them long to string the pieces together. We need to disappear, but not before we get you back to The Spa for your debrief."

How the hell does he know about debriefing procedures? Jewels thought to herself.

"Problem is I broke procedure and that'll have everyone on DEFCON five."

"Who is 'they'?" Jewels asked point blank.

"Your handlers," Todd told her.

"And what about *your* handlers?" Field inquired.

"That's an unknown," Todd answered. "They know I broke protocol, but they don't know why. That'll have them worried—maybe worried enough to buy us some time."

"Time for?" Fields asked.

"To figure out a plan."

"Why did you do it?" Jewels interrupted, looking Todd directly in the eyes.

He simply told her the truth. "Because I'm in love with you."

Jewels felt the air rush out of her lungs. This stranger had swooped into her life out of nowhere, and since the day they'd met, she hadn't been able to stop thinking about him. In fact, he'd been just about all she'd been able to think about. As hard as she'd tried, she couldn't get him out of her mind. She'd tried convincing herself, at worst, she'd had a schoolgirl crush on him, but as she heard him say the words, she knew she'd fallen for him as well. Without thinking, she was halfway over the front seat, both arms wrapped around him, burying her head into his neck, squeezing for all she was worth. He did the same, and for a few precious moments, the world melted away.

Samantha and Fields looked at one another, feeling the energy between Jewels and Todd. It was undeniable. The problem was they were sitting in the middle of a dark parking lot with a bullseye on their collective asses.

Fields, still very much in the dark and uncertain as to her role in this whole scheme, didn't like the fact they were literally sitting ducks. She asked Samantha where The Spa was, and when hearing it was in Newport, it sent a little chill up her spine. *Steel*, she thought to herself as she started the car.

Hearing the motor turn over, Todd looked up. "Heading to Newport," Fields told him, receiving his nod of approval.

On the way to Newport, between them all, they actually came up with a plan. Talk about making God laugh.

Chapter 11

Heading south on the 405, Fields had her vehicle's communication systems on scan, expecting the worse, and surprisingly, at least to her, hearing no unusual chatter. But Todd knew better. The powers they were dealing with didn't talk. No warnings. They just acted, striking with lethal force and never leaving a trace.

During the drive, Jewels reached her long-time driver, Darryl, and apologized for getting away from the party in such a rush, explaining that James had had too much to drink and freaked out about being seen on the news intoxicated, so they'd gotten a ride out of the mess with a friend of Todd's.

There was only a handful of limos left at the party when he received her call. He'd been in the dark. With no GPS on her beaming into the limo's coms from her phone, he'd been waiting patiently, along with all the other divers, for a call from the head valet when each respective limo party was ready for pickup. Hearing directly from Jewels was unexpected. He didn't give a shit about her explanation but was upset about her being in another vehicle. In transit, she was his responsibility, and he took his job very seriously. He and Jewels made arrangements for the vehicles to meet at the furthest end of the lower deck, arriving flights, at John Wayne Airport.

"This time of night, the place will be all but deserted," she assured Todd.

He agreed, nodding. "No way to say this than just straight up," he said after the rendezvous was set. "If the president ejaculated during your encounter," doing his best to phrase things as delicately as possible, "they're going to want proof."

"What?" Jewels asked innocently, still not having a clue as to the depth of shit they were in.

"They want a sample of his DNA," Todd told her.

"Why?"

"As proof of his . . . affair."

"What affair?" Jewels snapped back defensively. "The asshole came up behind me and practically raped me."

Everyone was silent hearing that.

"Irrelevant," Todd finally said factually. "What happened, how it happened, you, me, none us matter. The only thing they want is proof, and that proof, if there is any, is inside you."

Realizing the depth of what he was inferring sent Jewels over the edge. "I think I'm going to puke," she said, lowering the window as an uncontrollable wave of nausea swept through her entire body.

Samantha held her hair back as they continued flying south on the 405 with Jewels' body trying to expel the entire experience all over the outside of Fields' car.

***

Todd looked over at Fields, who was still very much on the fence with this entire ordeal.

"We need a twenty-four-hour emergency vet," Todd said, looking at her.

Fields nodded her head, reaching for the computer screen mounted inside her vehicle. "All I can say is, you'd better be for real."

***

In route, Fields' onboard computer had the facility. Todd called ahead, speaking with the on-duty veterinarian, who agreed to meet him at the rear door to the clinic, provided Todd had bona fide proof confirming who he said he was. Todd inquired about the clinic's security system. "Old school," the vet told him. "We have one camera in the reception room, that's it."

Twenty minutes later they were exiting off Bake Parkway and pulling into the back entrance of the Irvine 24-Hour Vet-Care Clinic.

"Jewels, please, you have to trust me," Todd pleaded, coming back to the car.

"Trust you," Jewels asked despairingly, shaking her head in disbelief at what had transpired in the past sixty minutes.

"It's the only chance we have of staying alive."

I'm in love with a total stranger that's worried we might not live through the night. Surrendering her fate to destiny, she smiled at Todd, took a deep breath, and said, "Then let's get this done."

***

Other than a tech, there was no one else working the clinic, *which is spotless*, Jewels thought thankfully to herself as they walked into the clinic's small operating room. The stainless-steel examination table glistened in the cold, circular halogen light above it.

Seeing Jewels' reaction, Samantha immediately asked the doctor, "Can you please get us a sterile sheet and some clean towels, anything to put down on the table?"

"Absolutely," the young vet answered, "I'll be right back."

Todd followed him out of the room and into the hallway. "Just to confirm, we need samples of everything present."

"Understood," the vet assured Todd, nodding.

"And equally as important," Todd told the young vet, bearing directly into his eyes, "you'll need to flush her clean."

"Understood."

Todd reached out, his hand across the top of the vet's arm, stopping him from reaching for the linen closet. "Absolutely no foreign fluids or trace chemicals. She's got to test like a virgin when we leave here."

Taken aback, the vet stared at this stranger who'd shown up in the middle of the night with three beautiful young women, two dressed to the nines, and a third that looked like a cop, telling him this was a matter of national security and they were never here. "Won't be a problem," the vet finally managed to get out. "Once I've swabbed her, I'll use a saline solution."

"Salt based?" Todd confirmed.

"Yes. One-hundred-percent natural, no chemicals. Then I'll flush with fresh water. She'll be clean as a whistle."

"Thank you, son," Todd said sincerely, putting a handful of Franklins in the vet's scrubs' side pocket.

"That's not necessary," the vet told him.

"I know," Todd said, "but your government appreciates your help and, equally as important, your discretion."

The vet nodded.

"As hard as this is to believe, it's truly a matter of the highest security."

Wackos, the vet thought, pulling out a couple of sterile sheets.

***

Leaving the clinic with a small Igloo cooler filled with blue ice, they continued south, meeting Darryl at the airport. James was still passed out in the back seat, oblivious to the world, but Darryl and Todd were able to manhandle him into the limo, leaving the rest of the troop standing outside the vehicles in the cold, silent wee hours of the morning.

The men stepped away from the others. They were both experienced professionals. Looking hard at one another, Todd extended his hand and said, "Thank you for taking such good care of her."

Darryl nodded slowly as Todd continued.

"I'm sorry for pulling her out from under you."

Darryl nodded again slightly.

"Under the circumstances I didn't have any choice. I had to get her out of there."

There was a long pause before Darryl said, "Then thank you for taking care of her."

Todd nodded this time. After a beat Darryl asked, "What about him?" gesturing his chin toward James in the back of the limo.

"If you could swing by the hotel on your way back to the spa, I'll let them know you're coming and there will be someone waiting curbside to help you with him. They'll take care of him from there. He practically lives in that place, and he's been dropped off like this more than a few times."

"Anything to worry about?" Darryl asked.

"No. Nothing. He's hammered and won't remember a thing when he wakes up."

"Okay then," Darryl said as both men walked back toward the vehicles.

Sensing they needed to talk, Darryl stepped away from the rear door of the limo he'd been holding open for Jewels and got behind the wheel, closing his driver's door. The limo's glass partition was up.

Todd felt fear through Jewels' hands as she held onto his arm. "It's going to be okay. We're almost through this," he said, trying to convince her, knowing full well it was only the beginning. "Just follow protocol. We'll be waiting when you come out."

Jewels shook her head. To this point, she'd been able to handle everything because Todd was with her. Realizing she had to move forward from here without him, she started to freak. "I can't do this without you," Jewels pleaded, squeezing his arm tighter.

"You can," Todd told her, looking into her eyes. "I'm not going anywhere. Samantha will be with you."

Jewels shook her head no.

"You've been through these hundred times. Be strong. It's critical we follow protocol—nothing out of the norm. They know something went sideways, but they don't know why. This will buy us a little time, giving them what they want."

Jewels didn't say anything. There was nothing she could say. Instead, she pushed her head into his chest. He held tight.

"When you walk out of there, I'll never leave again."

"Promise?" she murmured without lifting her head.

"I promise."

Taking a deep breath and mustering all the courage she had left in her being, she said, "Okay let's do this." Reaching up, she took Todd's head in her hands, pulling his face to hers for their first kiss.

Fields and Todd followed the sleek black limo back to The Spa, pulling off as Darryl entered the garage. The girls were met in the garage by several immaculately dressed armed men. *Unusual,* Jewels thought to herself. Getting out of the limo, another bolt of fear surging through her. *Breathe . . . just breathe,* she told herself. Unexpectedly, one of the men reached out politely, taking Samantha's arm, asking her to go with him while the other two positioned themselves on either side of Jewels.

"What's going on?" Jewels asked.

161

"Standard procedure, ma'am," one of the men told her.

"Bullshit," Jewels snapped back at him, attempting to step away from her guards towards Samantha. "There's nothing standard about this."

"You're right, ma'am," he said, nodding his head. "It's been an extraordinary evening, and if you will please just come with us while we escort your friend up to your dressing room." It wasn't a request.

"I'm fine," Sam offered lamely, even though her legs felt weak, pulling her arm away. "Jewels, I'll see you in a few minutes, girl."

With that, the ladies were individually escorted into separate elevators, Samantha being taken, as promised, to the dressing room, while Jewels was escorted to an examination room. Even though she'd been through the procedure hundreds of times before, this time was different. Instead of just the single technician, there were several. Meticulous attention was being paid to every detail, Coupled with the incredible intensity in the room, everything became surreal. When the technicians each took several vaginal swabs instead of the normal singular swirl, it hit her. *Todd has been right all night. They want his DNA . . . whoever the hell they are.*

***

Samantha changed out of her evening gown and back into the clothes she'd walked into The Spa wearing in what now felt like a lifetime ago. She'd been patiently waiting for over an hour. Jewels came out of the steaming hot shower, a towel wrapped tightly around her breasts, another in her hand patting dry her hair. Their eyes met. Neither said a thing. The women sat silently together in the deserted locker room.

Eventually, Jewels said, "I'm so sorry I dragged you into this mess."

"Don't be," Sam responded. "I'm okay. Just worried about how you're doing."

Jewels shook her head slowly. "I don't know what's going on, but whatever it is, it scares me to death." She looked at her friend. "But the strangest thing is, I can't remember ever feeling more alive in my life."

Samantha squeezed her friend's hand as Jewels continued. "I'd gotten to the point where I'd accepted the fact I'd never find anyone that makes me feel the way Todd does, but . . ."

Samantha, knowing all truths follow the "but," allowed her friend to continue exploring her thoughts without interrupting.

"I know this sounds so selfish and indulgent, but all I want to do is run away with him and never look back."

Samantha understood, nodding while remaining silent.

"How any of this happened is beyond me," Jewels continued, trying to make sense of it all. "Up until tonight, it's all pretty much been fun and games—honestly, nothing more than just a job. But tonight . . . everything changed."

"It's been an interesting night," Sam agreed, "to say the least."

"I'd say," Jewels said, standing up, flicking back her hair and pulling on an oversized hoodie. She was starting to feel somewhat normal again by dressing in comfort clothes and in the quiet, secure surroundings of her dressing room.

"In addition to who was involved," Jewels continued, rolling her eyes because both women knew no experience involving the president of the United States was ever going to be normal, "the night, the entire operation, you being here, the whole deal, was different."

She paused again, going over every detail of her encounter, frame by frame, in her mind. "The fact Todd seemed to know

what was happening almost before it even happened baffles me."
She shook her head. "The fact that he was my assignment—or
at least I thought he was my assignment right up till the minute
that huge guy took me into that room . . ." Her voice trailed off.
"Todd was right there beside me in the hall. The next thing I
knew he was gone, and I was being shoved into this dark room."

Their eyes met again.

Jewels shook her head. "I never saw him."

"Who? The president?" Samantha asked, taken aback.

"Yeah," Jewels confirmed. "I never saw him. One minute
I'm standing there, and the next thing I knew, he came up from
behind and was all over me. Obviously, he'd been waiting for
me," Jewels continued, playing back the scene in slow motion,
trying to make sense of what happened.

"So, you never talked to him?"

"Not a word. He slapped my ass, calling me a fucking whore.
He had a hard-on when he came up behind me. He grabbed my
breasts, bit my neck, pulled my hair, ripped down my panties,
bent me over the side of a chair, and jammed it in."

Samantha nodded.

"He was pissed off and didn't give a shit about me. I've never
felt a man fuck me with such pure hatred. It was so scary. Then
all of a sudden, we're crashing to the floor."

Samantha was speechless.

"The next thing I knew, Todd was there, helping me up,
saying we had to get out of there."

***

"Well, whomever you are, Mr. Highest Priority-One Clearance
in the world," Fields inquired after the girls' limo slipped into the
garage, "you come up with a plan yet?"

Todd looked over at her. She'd impressed him thus far with her professionalism, instincts, and most of all her ability to observe details and react while keeping her mouth shut. Instead of answering, he asked what her assessment of the situation was.

"Not a fair question," she answered immediately, "given I know virtually nothing about *the situation*."

Todd nodded. "You're absolutely right." He paused before continuing. "First of all, thank you."

Fields nodded in appreciation of him saying so. "Did I have a choice?"

"Multiple," Todd told her.

She nodded, knowing full well she could have reacted a thousand different ways, every one a choice. "I'm still here with you, so if you wouldn't mind, maybe try and at least fill me in."

"Besides the obvious?" Todd asked, shaking his head as if he was still trying to come to terms with what he'd done.

"That you've got yourself, and apparently all of us, into a jackpot."

Looking her in the eye, he said, "It's a thousand times worse than you can even imagine."

"I've got a pretty vivid imagination."

"My suggestion is that you forget we ever met, tell me to get out of your car, and drive yourself back into your life."

"Possibly the smartest idea you've had a night, but I don't think so."

"Why not?"

"The way I see it," Fields told him, "whatever made you do what you did has to be pretty goddamned important."

Todd nodded.

Fields waited, but no further explanation was offered. "Okay, then I'm in."

"Why?"

"Because I've been at this for over a dozen years and, honestly, what I've done hasn't made the least bit of a difference."

Nodding he understood her frustration, she continued, "Plus, there's something rotten in Denmark."

A small grin formed on Todd's lips. "Yeah, there's some rotten shit going on."

"If I can help you break it, then I'm all in."

Roughly thirty minutes later, Fields knew she'd found the asset she'd been looking for, hoping for, in Todd. After hearing the Cliffs Note version of her history lesson she'd laid out during lunch with Steel, Todd began filling her in on details way above her pay grade—or for that matter above anyone else's in government, including the president, facts she couldn't have even imagined possible, facts that put a bow around her theory and left her speechless.

***

With footage of the president in hand, things were heating up. The Elites had the deadly ammunition they had not managed to obtain since the man had taken office. His isolation had been impenetrable. In over a hundred years, they'd never had to deal with a more paranoid target, a target they had to bring under control one way or the other before it was too late. Even though his second term was coming to an end, they knew he and his cartel had no intentions of losing any control. He'd already laid the groundwork for causing more harm to this country, to the world order, than any other single man since Hitler. He had to be stopped.

***

Glancing down at the Igloo on the floor in front of Todd, Fields stated the obvious. "We need to get some tissue samples to forensics, and I'm assuming it's got to be off the record."

Todd nodded. "It's the only thing we have right now that's keeping us alive."

"Assuming there's any DNA to be had," Fields added, vocalizing Todd's worries, "and our young vet was able to get samples before he cleared any trace of contributors."

Todd shook his head at the absurdity of it all. Formulating a plan based on a prayer that a young, unknown veterinarian was able to capture any nuclear evidence to begin with, and then sanitize Jewels without leaving any markers, this was not how he was accustomed to doing business. In fact, it was pushing the polar opposite.

"I have a friend," Fields offered, "here in Newport that might be willing to help."

"Local PD?" Todd asked.

Fields nodded.

"Can you trust him?"

She shrugged her shoulders. "Not sure. Chances are it'll depend on—"

"If he believes us?"

"Pretty much," she confirmed, adding, "I like him. Good police. But we just met and haven't even worked a case."

"Hmm."

"Good news," Fields added, "he listened to my history spiel the other day and didn't arrest me for having escaped from the loony bin with all my speculations."

Todd looked intently at her and asked, "Why did you decide to run it by him?"

Fields answered honestly, "I like him. I wanted another set of eyes on it, and obviously there's no one inside the agency I'd ever consider telling."

"What was your take?"

"He's got great instincts, a nose for the truth, and once he's on the scent, a pit bull."

"What about your theory?"

"Like I just told you, he didn't arrest me."

"You want to call him?"

***

Twenty minutes later, Steel pulled up next to Fields and Todd, driver's side door to driver's side door, giving Fields a nod, his attention focused on Todd.

The two professionals assessed one another instantly. After a few beats, Steel refocused on Fields. "What's up?"

Fields glanced over at Todd before stating flat-out, "We need your help."

A few minutes later she'd summed up the evening as best she could. She and Todd then both waited in silence for his response.

Glancing at his watch, Steel finally said, "It's almost four. Give me the samples and I'll walk them into the lab. Our tech comes in at five."

Todd handed over one of the two sample tubes without hesitation, knowing Steel was their only option. He was either going to do it or fry them.

"Getting the samples digitized won't be a problem. But you know as well as I do, getting them tagged and logged in is a whole other issue."

"We don't need them recorded," Todd said. "We just need the results."

"Under a John Doe," Steel added.

Todd nodded.

"Meet me at the Galley at nine, and I'll give you the thumb drive."

"Can't," Todd said, nodding towards Jewels and Samantha as they stepped out from the garage entrance. "We need to get them out of here now."

Steel didn't want to be seen by the women.

Seeing the two vehicles parked together, Jewels reached over, touching Sam's arm. "Let's wait here for a minute."

Sam looked inquiringly at her.

"They know we're here," Jewels continued. "Let's give them a minute and see what happens."

Seeing the women stop, all three officers were impressed. "Talk about instincts," Fields commented.

"What about you?" Steel asked Fields. "Are you compromised?"

"I don't think so, at least not as of right now," she told him. "All SOP thus far, as far as my boss is concerned. He doesn't know shit other than I was on duty and released after POTUS left the building. He doesn't know where I am or whom I'm with."

"Until they realize you're the ones who stole their sacred lamb," Steel said.

"How long?" Fields asked.

"A few hours at best," Todd told her. "Then the shit is going to hit the fan, and we'll be facing the wrath of God."

"May I make a suggestion?" Steel offered, filling in the blanks on his own.

"Please," Todd responded.

"Get up to Long Beach. Catch the express to Catalina. They have ferries leaving every couple of hours. Split up. Pay cash. You and Fields board as a couple and," he continued, nodding across the street towards the women, "have them board together. No IDs required, and no one there will even look twice."

Todd and Fields looked at one another.

169

"When you get there," Steel continued, "you two, not the girls, have the shore boat run you out to my boat. Catch it at the end of the green pier. My boat is on mooring two twenty-five. A few years back, I helped the couple that owns it out of a jam, and they've given me permission to be on the can for the season, so I leave my boat there all summer. I let friends use it from time to time, so nothing unusual about guests going aboard without me. Harbor Patrol there is cool." He paused "Have either of you spent any time around boats?"

For the first time since pulling Jewels out of that room, Todd smiled, if only to himself, thinking, *If he only knew.*

"I've had some time on boats." Todd answered flatly.

"Can you handle a hard-bottom inflatable? Start a generator? The basics?"

"Anything special I need to know about her?" Todd asked.

"No," Steel continued. "She's dark right now. Main battery switches are on the aft bulkhead in the engine room. Start the gen up on both, then switch to either bank, one or two, it doesn't matter."

"Preheat switch on the starting panel?" Todd asked.

Steel nodded, realizing maybe Todd did know a little something about boats. "Just flip the main control from Off to House, and you'll be good to go. I leave the panel set, but every breaker is clearly labeled if you need power to anything else.

"Fuel?"

"Topped off. Key for the inflatable is under the center console."

"What about the girls?" Fields asked.

"When they get off the ferry, tell them to just walk into town along with everyone else. Maybe grab something to eat, then continue all the way around the harbor. There's a dinghy dock directly in front of the casino. Tell them to wait along the seawall there. You'll be able to see them from the boat, then run the dinghy in and pick them up."

"What about you?" Fields asked, looking Steel directly in the eyes.

"I'll pick up the lab results and catch the nine a.m. flyer out of Newport. I'll be there around ten fifteen."

"Want us to pick you up?"

"No, I'll take the shore boat like I usually do. Once I'm there and we know the lab results, we can figure out what to do next."

"How big is the boat?" Todd asked.

"Sixty." Steel told him.

"And her name?"

"*Vintage*."

***

As Steel pulled away, the girls crossed the street and got in the car. Instead of heading north up the dark deserted Pacific Coast Highway towards Long Beach, Todd instructed Fields to get onto Jamboree heading east. Without asking why, she drove them right past the front of the NBPD headquarters before making a right onto Jamboree. Todd was on his cell.

"Sorry to wake you," he said softly, "but we're ten minutes out."

"Understood," was all he needed to hear as he ended the call.

After a long silence, Fields asked, "Ten from where?"

"Orange County airport."

"Why are we going back there?" Samantha asked.

"We need to drop these off," Todd said, holding up his phone, "before we try and disappear."

Fields stared at him long enough to make Todd nervous about her not having her eyes on the road.

"It's our only play," he explained, nodding towards the front of the car. "Not only our phones, but this vehicle and most likely Ms. Jewels herself has at least one chip embedded in her body somewhere."

"What," cried Jewels from the back seat, "are you talking about?"

"I'm not a hundred percent on this," he said, turning around facing her, trying to sound reassuring, "but you've become far too valuable an asset for them not to have installed one."

Looking down, her hands immediately, instinctively ran down her arms and legs, desperately feeling for anything unnatural.

"You'll never feel it," he continued. "Thin. As thin as a kitten's whisker."

Jewels' complexion faded as the sheer terror of what was happening, not only to her but possibly inside of her, began to overwhelm her.

Todd reached back, taking her hand, drawing her attention. "It's going to be okay," he said, looking directly into her eyes.

She just shook her head as her eyes dropped to the floor.

"I'm assuming you haven't booked us on the first commercial flight out of here," Fields asked sarcastically, causing an ever so slight of a smile to crease his lips as he turned away from Jewels.

"Paragon," he said flatly.

***

Paragon started out in a small hanger office at John Wayne Airport in 2005 with a folding table and two chairs. Since then, it has grown into one of the busiest, multi-aircraft private charter jet services in the world. Landing The Spa as a client was Paragon's touchstone toward it's metamorphic rise and success. Due in no small part to Todd's lifelong friendship with the founder, who still flew from time to time, he was waiting for them with the gate open, and they silently drove through and around the front of the deserted hanger.

"Agent Fields?" Todd asked softly.

This was a moment that would determine the rest of her life. She knew she'd have to pay for what she'd done already. Her mind raced. She hadn't broken any laws, but by breaking protocol and not reporting in, there was going to be hell to pay.

Todd never took his eyes off her. Watching intensely as she weighed her options, he remained silent. This was her call and her call alone.

Without saying a word, she pulled her phone from her pocket, pulled the battery out, and handed it to him. He nodded.

"Ladies," he said, turning towards Jewels and Samantha. They both already had their phones out and handed them to him. The girls both had iPhones, so he placed them on the flat surface of the dashboard to pull their batteries out. His and Agent Fields' both were Androids, so their batteries came out easily.

"So they can't be traced?" Samantha asked.

Todd nodded.

"It's not enough to just turn them off?"

"Switched-off phones are actually in sleep or standby mode. Airplane mode with radio off doesn't prevent them from being traced."

"Seriously?"

"Most people believe no radio, no trace, which law enforcement wants the public to believe, but that's not the case. There are trap doors or spyware that can trace a phone even in airplane mode."

"What about those chip things I see guys breaking on TV?"

Todd smiled. "We'll be fine so long as the batteries are out and we keep them cold," he said, referring to the Igloo ice chest.

"I'm so sorry about all this," Jewels murmured under her breath to her best friend.

"Don't be," Samantha assured her. "I just learned something new. No matter what happens, we're in this together."

Jewels squeezed her hand.

Todd got out of the car as the owner stepped into the dim glow of the Citation V's taillights. The men hugged.

"Thanks," the ladies heard Todd say.

The owner nodded.

"I mean it, thank you."

"My pleasure," his lifelong friend told him. "Whatever you need."

Handing him the phones, Todd said, "We're gone or we're dead."

The owner nodded he understood. "I'm taking her myself," he said, nodding towards the beautiful jet. "Figured the fewer the better."

"Once you're airborne, log your flight plan as a Spa charter with me and three unknown females. Head to Kauai," Todd said, "but don't land. Approach the island at regular altitude, but then glide in behind the mountains. You'll fall off their radar. Stay low, bank west, and head for Midway."

"Tower is going to wonder what the fuck happened."

"Out of the ordinary for sure, but without a crash, they'll let it go, figuring just another rich asshole changing his mind at the last minute."

"They'll write it up."

"For sure, but no one's going to give a shit—at least not until you're long gone. By then it won't matter."

Calculating his fuel burn and range, the owner-pilot looked up. Todd had already done the math. "With no load, you'll have enough."

"Not by much," the pilot agreed, coming to the same conclusion.

"Even with a head wind, topped off, she carries enough to get you there safely."

"That runway hasn't been used in years."

"Not true," Todd. "No military activity, no regular commercial flights, but Air Phoenix has had the maintenance contract over there ever since the Navy pulled out in 1993. The runway is in perfect condition, very safe. Part of their deal. You'll be able to refuel there as well."

"Henderson Field," the pilot said softly.

"Roger. They renamed it after the Navy left," Todd continued. "The place is a national marine refuge managed by Fish and Wildlife, but the island's infrastructure is maintained by a small contingency from Sri Lanka. They maintain the generator plants, the airport, run all day-to-day operations."

Handing the pilot one of his cards, Todd instructed him to give it to whomever met the plane. "Tell him it's an emergency and you need to get topped off immediately."

Taking the card from Todd, he glanced at it. "Assuming there won't be any questions?"

"None. All part of their contract. That island is the most remote populated land mass on the planet, and as part of the deal when the Navy pulled out, we made sure that the runway and terminal were user ready if and when needed. In exchange for maintaining the air facilities there, they get to run eco tours and such shit, and we get a runway capable of handling the biggest we fly."

"Got it."

"When you arrive, there's going to be a small freighter, more like a shallow draft supply ship, at the mole. The ship circumnavigates those atolls, making its rounds once a month. It'll be there when you land."

"How do you know all this?" the pilot asked without thinking, amazed at his friend's ability to have a handle on so many details at once.

Todd glanced at him. "You don't want to know."

"What about the ship?"

"While the ground crew is refueling the jet, ask to borrow one of their jeeps, run one of these phones, and," he said, handing the pilot a thick roll of hundred-dollar bills, "give it and the money to the skipper."

"He won't be suspicious?"

Todd just shrugged. "Irrelevant. Doesn't matter. He won't be a problem. This is more money than he'll ever see in his lifetime."

"What do I tell him to do with the phone?"

"It doesn't matter. Whatever he wants to. Just turn it on before you give it to him and ask him to get it off the island when they depart. By the time the bad guys figure all this shit out, we'll be long gone." Todd answered.

"Got it."

"When you get back, turn these other three phones back on and just drop them somewhere in the terminal before you take off."

"For?"

"Islas Secas."

"That little island off Panama?"

"That's the place. Leave the plane, and they'll fly you to San Jose in one of the resort's private planes. Routine. They commute back and forth daily. Jump on a commercial flight back to the States. Twenty-four hours from now, if everything goes as planned, no one will be the wiser."

"One can only hope."

"You had mechanical issues at the island, and it was going to be several days before they could get a mechanic out to look at her."

176

"And rather than just relaxing at one of the premier resorts in the world, I decided to take a commercial flight home because we were so busy."

"Exactly. Wait a few days and you can have someone fly her home for you and take your wife down and spend a few days. It's all on my tab." Holding up the ice chest with the second vile from the vet, Todd added, "Don't let this out of your site." He handed it to him.

Taking it, the pilot nodded that he understood.

"If shit goes sideways, what's in there is your get-out-of-jail-free card."

"I'm assuming I don't want to know what's in there."

"You wouldn't believe me if I told you."

***

Todd looked over at the car, nodding to Jewels, signaling with his hand for her to join them. As she did, he told the pilot they needed the plane for a minute.

Stepping into the magnificent interior of the jet, Jewels would have been in awe except for the circumstances.

"I hate to have to do this," Todd told her in his most compassionate voice, "but I need to scope you."

"What?"

Pulling something out of his pocket that looked like it belonged in some futuristic space movie, he said, "If they chipped you, we've to get it out."

"You said you weren't sure they implanted one."

"I'm not, but if it was me, I would have." Pausing, he continued, "It'll only take a minute."

Jewels held out her arms like she'd seen a million times on TV.

"Afraid not," he said. "I have to look inside you."

"What?"

"Inside you," he said, lowering his eyes toward her private parts.

It only took her a second to realize what he was inferring. "You're kidding me."

"Sorry."

Surrendering, she asked mockingly, "Promise it won't hurt?" Taking off her pants, then pulling her panties down, she sat on the edge of one of the plush leather seats and opened her legs.

"I'm really sorry I have to do this," Todd said.

Jewels closed her eyes as Todd turned on his magic wand.

Less than ten seconds later, he removed the decoder. Holding it up in the light for her to see, it was barely visible, but sure as shit, in the tiny, tweezer-like tip of the device was what looked like a razor-thin strand of short hair.

"Unbelievable," Jewels murmured.

Todd carefully dropped the tiny tracking device into a small, clear vile.

"Where do you get all this shit?" Jewels asked, still not believing what he'd just pulled out of her body.

Todd forced a smile, avoiding her question. "Didn't hurt at all, did it?" he asked.

But she'd anticipated what was next.

"Sorry" he said. "I really am, but we have to be sure."

Slowly, she rolled over onto her stomach, allowing him to examine her anal cavity.

"Knew it," he mumbled under his breath, pulling out another thin wire tracker. *Motherfuckers*, he thought to himself.

With her face still down, facing away from him, she asked in a schoolgirl's voice while pulling up her pants and panties, "Are we done playing doctor? Do I get a lollipop now?"

"Almost," Todd answered, dropping the second tracker into the vile. "Say ahhhh." That was followed by a look up her nose and into each ear.

"A quick scan through your beautiful mane and we'll be done." He moved the sensing device through her hair as he spoke, finding one more unit implanted just below her hairline on the back of her neck. "Okay, you're clean," he announced.

Watching him drop the last tiny tracker into the vile, Jewels asked, "Why didn't my body reject these things. Even as small as they are, they're still foreign material. Wouldn't it be like having a little splinter or something? Especially down there. Gives me the creeps."

"Short version. They combine stem cells with your own DNA and encapsulate the chips. The body accepts the cells as its own and allows them to naturally adhere to the lining of the soft tissue."

"How?"

"From DNA they collect during your routine, post-assignment swabs."

"Are you kidding me?"

"Afraid not. It's some pretty advanced science."

"You think?"

"Let's go."

Todd paused, looking at her. She managed a thin smile, instantly returned. Before he could turn away, she reached up, both hands gliding around his neck, pulling his mouth to hers. Their second kiss on what she was now pretending to be their first date.

*****

Outside the plane, Todd added the vile with all three of Jewel's tracers to the ice chest. "Pull this one out when you get to PTY.

Keep it in your pocket, then drop it in a trashcan just before you board the plane to come home."

"What about the ice chest?"

"Leave it at the airport."

"Open or closed."

"Open it, so if anyone looks in, they won't be suspicious—just another little cooler with some melted ice that someone left behind."

With that, the two men hugged one another again. The pilot had the boarding ladder closing and was pulling the beautiful sleek jet away from the hanger as Fields turned the car around.

The girls remained silent as they drove away into the darkness.

"Let's get back on PCH and head north," Todd told Fields as he went over the plan he and Steel had come up with.

Again, silence.

"Okay," he admitted, "it's not much of a plan, but it should buy us a little more time."

"If we're lucky," Fields added, pushing the accelerator down as they sped north in the grey light of predawn.

Chapter 12

Todd knew what would be unfolding in certain departments within certain Federal agencies, including in the den of the president's Untouchables, as well within the secret halls of Todd's other employer, the Elites. It was a shit storm.

***

The very foundation of a democratic society, its lifeblood and sustainability, lies in the law and order that governs the land, an integrated, powerful system of checks and balances, an obedience to those laws and to the respective chains of command that enforce them. Break rank and consequences will be paid. Choices are free—the consequences of those choices, not so much.

While driving, one doesn't have to stop at a red light. No one is actually inside your vehicle forcing you to put your foot on the break. You break voluntarily, doing so because you know if you don't and decide to run the light, you could possibly sail through the intersection scot free, no harm, no foul. Or you could get caught and get a ticket. Or you could cause an accident, perhaps even kill someone—a perfect stranger, a child, a loved one, or even yourself. Regardless, the choice is yours every single time you drive through an intersection. Run a red light, get caught, pay a fine. Run a red light, kill someone, go to prison. Punishment or the payment due is equal to the violation or crime. For every action, there is an equal and opposite reaction. That's why we stop at red lights. Checks and balances at the street level.

Within the halls of government, all branches of the military and within all law enforcement agencies, and even major corporations at the highest levels where only the few and the Elite breathe the air, break rank within those confines, or disobey orders, and the consequences are extreme. When a rogue act sends tremors through the most powerful men in the world, all bets are off. Threaten the very foundation upon which over the Elite rule, treason and death become synonymous—no questions asked, no lawyers, no courts, no trials, no media. It's checks and balances in the stratosphere.

***

Todd's actions were ground zero. Yet, as of this moment, not a breath about the incident had left the inner circles of power, both near and afar. So, as dawn broke, over three hundred million Americans were waking up, starting their Sunday mornings off like they had every Sunday for over a hundred years. Alinsky's handbook on controlling the masses was quietly at work. Ignorance is bliss.

But there was no bliss in the White House. The Untouchables were screaming for Todd's head. The charge was led by none other than the leader of the free world himself, who upon screening the video of the incident, flew into an uncontrollable rage, further inflaming his gonads, which had turned dark purple and were swollen to the size of grapefruits. The first lady herself was not too pleased by the situation either. In fact, she was boiling inside.

"You are such a fucking asshole!" she screamed at the commander in chief.

Her sentiments were shared by those in the inner circle, knowing all too well the president's political career was in the balance. They had no idea his life was at stake as well, because only the president himself knew that he'd betrayed his handlers, betrayed the very men that had put him in the White House. For the first time since being elected, the president of the United States was scared.

He knew he'd fucked up, and his handlers were men that did not tolerate mistakes. Even though he was on the way out of office after his second term, the groundwork had been carefully laid for the seamless transition of power to the first women ever publicly considered electable as president. Thanks to the endless support given to her by the mainstream media and the support of the untold billions of dollars expended by the handlers, she was a lock, assuring that they would maintain control of the country.

The president had been warned about this. He'd taken every precaution, built an entire presidential guard around him, his very own personal untouchables, to ensure he'd never be caught. Up until now.

"I want that asshole's head on a platter! He's a goddamned terrorist, motherfucking traitor," the president screamed. "In the executive powers invested in me by the Constitution of the United States, I hereby authorize every agency, every branch of the military, and every goddamned cop in this fucking country to shoot that motherfucker on sight!"

"Sir," one of his aides pleaded, "you can't do that."

"I can do whatever the fuck I want," he screamed. "I'm goddamned president of the fucking United States. Issue the fucking order! I want that asshole dead!"

***

Pulling up to the curb a block from the ferry terminal, Fields dropped the girls off, then drove offsite, pulling into a dimly lit underground garage, driving to the lowest level, and finding a parking spot as near to the middle of the structure as she could find. Todd nodded his approval, understanding why she chose this spot. She locked the vehicle before walking back to the docks with Todd. In just the fifteen minutes it had taken for them to park, the terminal had become a swarm of people, mostly tourists, anxious to get their trip started. The Four Preps 1958 song "Twenty-Six Miles Across the Sea" filled the air, welcoming passengers as they stepped onboard. They were all able to get seats on the first boat departing for the island. Pulling out of the breakwater, the sea was grease and the ride smooth and uneventful. With the fresh salt air filling their lungs, the trip over could have been described as soothing, except for the churning nerves within each of their souls. The girls sat together several rows in front of Fields and Todd. They never glanced back, knowing Fields and Todd had their backs.

***

Todd had the generator running and was getting familiar with the rest of the boat when Fields spotted the girls making their way to the seawall in front of the Casino. This was Fields' first time on the island, and she was overwhelmed seeing the architecture of the building. Moored less than a hundred feet from its base and looking up from the cockpit of the *Vintage*, the Casino's twelve stories towered overhead. Her mind drifted off point as she found herself curious to learn more about this fascinating building.

"Beautiful," she heard from behind her, startling her back to reality. She spun around, realizing a Harbor Patrol officer had silently slid his bright-red patrol boat up along their starboard side. "Your first time here," he continued.

"Yeah," Fields said, surprised that he'd been able to pull up without her noticing.

"Sorry if I startled you."

"No, no. That's okay," she said. "I was just looking at that building."

The officer smiled. "It's called the Casino. Completed in May 1929."

"It's beautiful," Fields said, still miffed at herself for having been caught off guard.

"Built by Bill Wrigley Junior," the patrolmen added.

"The Wrigley chewing gum family? Chicago?"

"One in the same. That was his house over there," the officer said, pointing directly opposite of the Casino across the bay towards a sprawling, gleaming-white mansion sitting alone atop the hill on the eastern slope overlooking Avalon. Within minutes, she learned more about the island, the Casino, and Avalon than she could imagine.

"The Cubs used to hold their spring training here, and Marilyn Monroe lived here when she was sixteen with her first husband. 310 Metropole, her house is still here."

Fields found herself totally absorbed with the officer's narrative. Todd came out from the salon and greeted the officer, introducing himself under a false name, reminding Fields why they were there and ending her little fantasy tour of Avalon history.

"Nice to meet you. Mind if I come on board?" he asked nonchalantly.

"Ahh," Todd paused, instantly on alert, "may I ask why?"

Shaking a small canister of orange dye tablets, the officer answered casually, "SOP. Just need to drop one of these in each head." Realizing neither of the boat's crew knew what he was talking about, he asked, "First time here?"

"It is," Todd said, extending his hand, helping the officer onboard.

"Thank you. We have a zero-discharge policy here. These little babies let us know if anyone is flushing their heads overboard."

"Understand," Todd answered. "But give me a minute to get below and double-check the valves."

"No problem," the officer said, smiling, looking at Fields and nodding politely. "We were just getting caught up on a little Avalon history."

It took Todd a little longer than expected, tracing the plumbing system under each of the heads, making sure they were all set to discharge into the holding tank and not overboard. He couldn't imagine Steel leaving the boat set in any other way, but the last thing they needed was to get busted for illegal discharge, as ironic as that might have been.

"All set," he announced, coming back into the cockpit where the history lesson had resumed.

"Such an amazingly quaint place," Fields told the officer. "Lived in LA for years, and I've never once been here."

"We hear that all the time," the officer said, smiling. "Hopefully, this won't be your last."

Todd led the officer to each head and, as requested, flushed each one after the officer dropped one or two tabs into each bowl.

"How many days are you planning on staying?" the officer asked as they returned to the cockpit.

On defense, Todd asked, "Why do you need to know?"

"Just want to get it in the logbook is all."

"Are there any fees?" Todd asked.

"Oh yeah, this boat is eighty-six dollars per day, but the owner has her paid up in full through the summer, so you guys are good to go," he said, effortlessly jumping back into his patrol boat. "Enjoy your stay."

Once again looking at Fields, before shoving off he added, "If you need anything, just give us a call on twelve."

"Will do," Fields said as they waved goodbye to the departing officer.

The girls had been silently watching from the seawall. Todd looked over at them, giving them a little thumbs up that everything was okay. Turning to Fields, he said, "Let's get the dinghy launched and go pick them up."

***

A few minutes later they had the girls safely on board. Everyone began getting orientated to the boat. It had a beautiful, full-width, master stateroom with a single king-size bed, its own head and shower, and tons of built-in teak cabinets. There were two identical guest staterooms, port and starboard, both with two single bunks, heads and showers, and a crew's quarters forward with a lower double and upper queen. The salon couch converted to sleep two more guests, and there was another queen berth located on the upper deck under the overhead of the enclosed wheelhouse, with an additional single berth inside the wheelhouse as well.

"This thing has more beds than a small roadside motel," Fields said.

"I counted fourteen," Todd told her.

Fields nodded in confirmation, adding, "Now what?"

There was silence. The extent of the plan had been to simply get to the boat. "Steel said to wait until he gets here," Fields said, breaking the silence. Everyone nodded in agreement.

"Okay, but how about we run into town, look around a little, maybe grab something to eat?" Jewels suggested. "I don't know about the rest of you, but I'm starving."

***

They all loaded into the fourteen-foot, center-console, hard-bottom, inflatable outfitted with a forty horsepower Suzuki four-stroke and made their way to the dinghy dock.

Once secured, they walked into town. Avalon is a unique little town, somehow magically captured in some sort of a time warp. Tiny shops dot the narrow streets, with European style cafes wedged between the shops selling Catalina trinkets to the tourists. It's hard not to fall in love with Avalon. They eventually settled in on some old wooden chairs surrounding an outdoor table covered with a clean red-and-white checkered tablecloth in front of one of the cafes located on one of the side streets and ordered breakfast.

None of them realized how hungry they were until they sat down. Adrenaline will do that, but once it wears off, all the body functions you've been ignoring start flooding back into play, demanding attention.

"I had no idea how hungry I was," Samantha said, breaking the comfortable silence that had settled over the table as they ate.

"Me too," Jewels confirmed, nodding at her friend before looking over at Todd. "So, what's next?"

Todd met her stare before shaking his head. "Honestly, I don't know."

"What we do next will all be based on the lab results," Fields chimed in, looking over at Todd, "or at least that's the way I see it."

"You're absolutely right," Todd confirmed. "Once we know what we have to work with, we plan from there."

The girls nodded, knowing that no matter what happened next, their lives would never be the same.

As they finished a delicious meal, Todd suggested, "I saw a Ralph's around the corner. Why don't we get some supplies for the boat?"

***

A little over an hour later, they'd practically cleared the shelves from the small grocery store, toted everything back down to the dinghy, and stored away close to two thousand dollars' worth of food, fresh perishables, frozen and dry goods, along with the last three prepaid disposable cell phones the store had.

"We could live off this stuff for a month if we had to," Jewels said, looking around at a now fully stocked boat.

"Hope we won't have to," Todd acknowledged, "but you're right. Worse case, we could get out of Dodge and be self-sufficient for a long time if we had to."

Jewels had been trying to put everything together, but there was so much she didn't know. Finally, she couldn't take not knowing any longer and blurted out, "Run from whom?"

Todd took a long deep breath, exhaling slowly. "From some very powerful people."

"That doesn't tell me shit," Jewels snapped back at him. "I deserve . . ." She stopped to look at Sam and Fields. "We all deserve to know what you've gotten us into."

Todd remained silent.

"Powerful people? What the hell does that mean?" Jewels demanded.

Another deep breath and Todd started trying to explain who he worked for. "Officially, I work for the federal government. head of the NSA."

"You're head of the National Security Council?" Fields asked in disbelief. Within the FBI and CIA, the head of NSA was considered a mystical figure, not an actual real person. No one person could ever handle having that much access—unlimited access—not even the president.

"You saw my credentials."

"Yeah," Fields answered. "It was dark, and all hell was breaking loose at that party. I glanced at it. Looked official enough to me. I certainly couldn't read what the fuck it said."

Todd smiled. "Trust me, it's real."

"I already have," Field added. The seriousness in her voice was not going unnoticed by anyone.

"And we're alive right now because you did," Todd said, looking her in the eyes. "I'll never forget what you've done." Continuing, he left nothing out.

Fields was the first to understand, or at least begin to understand the monumental, diabolic opposing forces they were in the middle of. It sent chills down her spine. She had to sit down. As Todd wrapped up his overview, Fields added, "Making individuals who jeopardize their agenda disappear means nothing to them."

"Correct," Todd confirmed.

"And from what I understand," Fields said, looking Todd in the eyes, "by pulling Jewels out of the party last night, you pretty much fucked up everyone's agenda. Torched both ends of the bridge, so to speak."

Todd nodded.

"Now you have nowhere to go. No one to turn to."

Todd slowly nodded again in agreement.

"If Steel's lab comes up positive for the president's DNA, and," Todd emphasized, "this is huge, The Spa's lab results come up negative for presidential DNA, then we at least have a bargaining chip."

"I'm sorry," Jewels asked softly, "but I still don't understand."

"In the simplest of terms," Todd continued, explaining, "I work—or at least I used to work—for both sides. One group wants to destroy the president's credibility by releasing the tapes from last night of you and him together."

190

"What tapes?" Jewels demanded.

"The FBI's closed-circuit surveillance feeds from every nook and cranny of that house last night."

"Fuck me," Jewels said, shaking her head.

"The bureau would never release those tapes," Fields said, defending her department.

"You're absolutely right," Todd agreed. "But the other men I work for have every frame of last night's coverage as well."

"No fucking way. That system is as secure as it gets," Fields rebutted.

"Come on," Todd pleaded, "the people I work for have unlimited funding. Nothing, and I mean nothing, is outside of their abilities, and scraping off a live feed, even an FBI encoded feed, isn't exactly rocket science. It's not even a challenge with the technology they have."

Starting to get angry for the first time since they'd met, Fields confronted him. "So, you work for the bad guys?"

Todd let the question sink in before answering. "I work for the United States of America," he said flatly.

"Bullshit!" Fields snapped at him. "The United States of America, that's not a fucking answer."

Todd closed his eyes before answering. "Fields, you know as well as I do that within every government, within every agency—hell, within every global enterprise—there are secretive, very powerful forces at work below the surface, and even subtler more powerful forces are in play behind those forces. Nothing is ever as it appears."

"And you're one of those forces?" Fields asked sarcastically.

He couldn't afford to lose her trust, so he came right out and asked, "What do you need me to tell you?"

"Who the fuck you're working for would be a good start."

"I told you. I'm head of the National Security Agency of the United States of America."

Fields shook her head. "If that was true, you'd never be in the field, not like this."

Todd nodded in agreement. "But we've never faced anything like this before."

"We . . ." Fields continued drilling suspiciously.

Todd let his gaze fall to the deck.

"And?" Fields demanded.

"I'm undercover in an organization known publicly as The Spa."

"What?" Jewels demanded. "You work for The Spa?"

"Head of security," Todd answered her honestly, "but I'm undercover."

"Bullshit. The background checks they run, they'd have known you work for the NSA."

"Absolutely. That's the beauty of the whole setup. They have no idea I'm a . . . in layman's terms, a double agent."

"So, this was all your idea?"

"No! No way, absolutely not," he said, reaching out touching her arm, which she immediately drew away. "I did everything I could to prevent the op from happening."

Tears formed in Jewel's eyes, shaking her head as the realization that the man she'd fallen in love with had actually been a part of her getting raped by the president.

"Jewels, please," Todd begged, looking at Fields, hoping for some help. "You're the reason I'm here, the reason I was at that fucking party. If I couldn't stop the op, I thought at least I could be there with you to prevent what happened from happening."

"Then you're not very good at your job," Jewels snapped. "Whatever that is."

"What does The Spa have to do with anything?" Fields asked.

Todd answered flatly, "Everything."

Just then, a bright yellow-and-white shore boat pulled up alongside the *Vintage*, and off jumped Sergeant Steel carrying what they all knew would determine the future of their lives.

Fields immediately threw her arms around him. "I'm so glad you're here," she whispered in his ear.

"Everything okay?" he asked suspiciously, looking around. He got tears and blank stares in return. "The ride over, the boat?" he added, buying time.

Todd nodded.

"Looks like you got her dialed in," Steel said, a little nod of approval at Todd. As Fields released her bear hug, he met Todd's eyes. Without being asked, he reached inside his coat pocket and handed the lab results to Todd.

Silence hung over the boat while Todd read the results. Looking up, meeting Steel's stare, he nodded.

"Well?" Jewels asked.

"We got it," Todd said softly.

"I'd say," Steel responded immediately. "The president's DNA, for Christ's sake," he continued, shaking his head. "The minute that dope came out this morning, it threw the entire department into a total cluster. The Feds were on us almost before we got the results. How the fuck does that happen?" he said, looking at Fields.

Shrugging her shoulders innocently, she shook her head. "I don't know."

"I jammed out the back door with that," he said, nodding towards the lab results Todd was still holding in his hand, "as they were storming the lobby." Pausing for dramatic effect, he added, "Along with this." He proudly held up the original vile from the vet's office.

"So, they've got nothing?" Todd asked, astonished.

"Other than the fact that the NBPD requested a standard lab test in the middle of the night that came back positive with the president of the United States' DNA, nope."

The men nodded subtly at one another before Steel added, "All I can say is this better be worth it, because we are all now officially in the middle of the fucking jackpot."

"Thank you," Todd said, reaching out to shake Steel's hand.

"Don't know you from Adam," he said, taking his hand. "I did it for her," he continued, looking Fields in the eye. Reaching out, he put his arms around her shoulder.

Her anger waning, realizing that everyone had put their careers, perhaps their lives, on the line for her, Jewels squeezed Todd's arm as Steel asked, "Got a plan?"

Slowly shaking his head no, Todd said, "We've been waiting for this. I need some time to think."

"I'm afraid that's something we don't have," Steel said, stating the obvious. "In all my years, I've never seen a department go sideways faster than it did this morning. The fucking Feds went ballistic," he said, looking at Fields. "No offense."

Fields assured him, "None taken."

Glancing around the boat, Steel could see that they'd been to the market. "How well stocked are we?" he asked.

"Enough to get by for at least a couple weeks."

"My suggestion is we mosey out of here. There are half a dozen secluded little coves with good anchorages on the backside. Not a lot of traffic on that side. That'll at least buy us some more time."

***

Within minutes, they'd dropped their mooring lines and were heading out of Avalon. As they rounded the east end and started up the backside, Steel knew exactly which cove he'd prefer to see vacant. Located about halfway up the island, he'd spent a couple weeks there last year.

"There's a little cove called Cottonwood just up a way. A little tricky getting into, but once inside, it's a deep, safe, well-protected anchorage. The best part, there's only enough room for one boat the size of *Vintage*."

***

As they rounded Church Rock, Jewels made her way forward and joined Samantha, who'd been sitting up on the bow since they'd left Avalon. "Hey."

"Hey," Samantha answered, squeezing Jewels' hand as she sat down beside her.

Neither felt the need to talk, each reflecting on the events of the past evening. The seas were still grease, no wind, no swell, as the *Vintage* nicely made her way north, up the backside of the island. The steady swooshing sound of the blue coming off her bow in an endless white curling wave of foam, blended peacefully with the strong, steady hum of her big CAT diesels, working together, soothing their souls in only the way of being on the open sea can do. No one on board had slept for over twenty-four hours, and as the last of the adrenaline drained from each individual's body, a false sense of well-being, a delusional high, was setting in.

"I couldn't write this shit," Samantha said quietly, breaking.

Jewel's focus had been on the beautiful V-shaped canyons cutting steeply through the island to the rocky edges of the shoreline, forming a perfect W. She looked at her friend, their eyes meeting as Samantha continued.

"Even if I could, no one would believe me."

Jewels smiled warmly. "So, you're thinking about making this into a movie?"

Sam shook her head, still trying to come to grips, to make sense of what's happening to them.

"We're going to be lucky if we live through the night, and you're thinking about writing a script?"

"That's what I do, girl," Sam answered. "That's who I am. Plus," she added honestly, "it helps me distance myself from what's actually happening to us, which I still don't think I even remotely understand."

Jewels paused before answering. "Maybe that's it. Maybe that's why you're here. I've been asking myself, why you? Maybe that's it. You're here so you can tell the world what happened."

Samantha didn't answer.

***

Up in the wheelhouse, things weren't quite as positive. The three seasoned law enforcement professionals were sitting in silence. The severe consequences of their recent decisions were weighing heavily on each of their minds.

Finally, Todd broke the silence. "First of all," he paused, waiting for both Steel and Fields to look at him, "Thank you. I want you both to know that if it hadn't been for you, Jewels would have never made it through the night." Steel and Fields nodded slowly. "The fact that you both put your asses on the line, well, I want you to know I'll never forget what you've done."

Steel had been gripping the wheel tightly ever since they'd left Avalon, even though the autopilot worked fine, and with flat seas, he could have been steering the boat with one finger. Having his hands wrapped around the worn, wooden helm gave him a sense of comfort, a sense of control in a world that was spinning out of control. "Like I said before, I did it for her."

Fields, sitting directly behind Steel in the helms seat, was standing in front of her with her arm around his waist, squeezing tightly.

"You know we're fucked," Steel added flatly.

"Not necessarily," Todd answered cautiously, getting a cold glance from both of them. They'd all spent their lives behind the shield and had seen far too much shit go down to think they had any chance of getting out of this clean.

"The entire federal government is after our asses," Steel stated flatly.

"Not to mention whomever else you shit on last night," Fields added.

"I know," Todd confirmed. "We're the bullseye of two of the most imposing forces on earth."

"You have to know how powerful the Feds are." Fields stated. "Hell, you're a part of it all."

Todd met her eyes, nodding he understood, adding, "I do. But they're a relatively slow-moving machine compared to what's coming at us from the other side."

Silence set in again.

Chapter 13

As they dropped anchor, backing down in the secluded little harbor, giving the boat plenty of scope before coming to, she settled nicely onto her new tether. They were the only boat there and, at least for a while, safe from any immediate danger.

"Let's splash the dinghy," Steel said. Looking astern at the shoreline less than thirty yards aft, he added, "It's a hike to get down to this beach from the island—only locals, and then only when there's a break. No swells, no visitors."

"What's up the hill?" Todd asked.

"Middle Ranch," Steel answered.

"A working ranch?"

"Yeah. There's three of them here on the island."

"Cattle?"

"The one up there runs some cattle," Steel said, pointing north. "It's a few miles inland from here. The other two, one boards horses, and the last one, I heard they're trying to create a vineyard."

"Seriously," Fields asked, "in this drought?"

"Yeah, I hear ya," Steel confirmed. "There's a big power struggle going on with the Island Company. The Wrigley heirs want to turn the place into a high-end destination, Newport style. The locals are fighting them all the way. I've heard they want to build a big resort up there with a private heliport, the works."

"Is there an airport on the island?" Todd asked.

"Sure is. They blew the top off a ridge back in the early 1930s to build it. Hasn't changed since."

"Assuming it's all private planes only?"

"Correct. Why?"

"Just wondering if a small jet could land there."

"I don't think so. Nearest runway that could handle a jet would be the base at San Clemente," Steel explained, nodding towards San Clemente Island off their port side.

"Military?"

"Yeah, Navy controls the island. Was fishing over there awhile back and watched a big ol' seven forty-seven transport doing touch and goes. It was cool watching 'em banking hard right over our heads, circling around and then coming back in, just touching down before putting full throttle to those babies and roaring off again. Went on for hours."

"Looks like it's about twenty miles from here," Todd said, looking at the island in the distance.

"Pretty close, more like eighteen." Steel paused, assessing Todd. "You thinking evac point?"

"More like escape options."

"What are we going to do?" Fields asked.

After a long pause, Todd took a deep breath. "This is a long shot, and I'm just flushing this out loud here. The president is on his way out, right?"

"Then why have your guys been so adamant about nailing him?"

"Because there's been talk about him staying in office."

"For a third term? That's insane. The Twenty-Second Amendment," Fields jumped in.

"Extenuating circumstances," Todd countered. "They've been running whatever bullshit they could come up with by legal internally, and they couldn't come up with anything other than we would have to be in a full-on state of war—and I mean full-blown nuclear war, not this ISIS bullshit—for it to possibly fly," Todd countered.

"Like Roosevelt."

"Exactly. Elected president four consecutive terms."

"What's interesting about that amendment," Fields added, "is it only made two-term presidents ineligible, and I quote, 'to be elected to the office of the president.' But if the standing president decides to run for vice president and his party wins and the newly elected president resigns or dies, then the VP, or old president, becomes the new president."

"That can't be right," Steel injected.

"Sure as shit," Fields said, quoting, "The Fifteen Amendment, Section One: In case of the removal of the president from office, or of this death or resignation, the vice president shall become president."

"So, in essence, you're saying the vice president is sworn in as president after the death of the president, even though he just served two terms as president, runs for re-election as vice president three years later and wins. The new president again resigns or dies, and the VP is sworn in as president?"

"Yep."

"And this could go on and on over and over again? That's insane," Steel said, stating the obvious.

"But they were thinking about it."

"Now it starts to make sense why your Elite wanted the goods on him."

"Correct. Insurance. I'm telling you there's a war raging that's going to determine the future of our country."

"They'd never get it passed."

"They wouldn't have to—executive order, national security. If they really wanted to, they could keep him in power for a long time, but they decided the consequences outweighed the benefits. So, a couple years ago they decided to move forward creating the first woman president."

"And exactly who the fuck are *they*?" Steel asked point blank.

"Best guess, it's a counter group, the mirror opposite to the Elites I'm undercover on."

"The chick's a lock," Steel injected. "She's up by fifteen points in the polls. Why are they so worried?"

"They've learned over the years that nothing is ever a lock. Take control and control the outcome."

Steel shook his head, looking back at Fields. "Like I said at lunch, way over my pay grade."

"I know how hard this shit is to imagine, but believe me, we're up against the most powerful men in the world. They have no alliances to any country, any government, no obligations to anyone other than themselves. We caught wind of all this a while back."

"How long ago?" Fields wanted to know.

"During the Clinton fiasco with Lewinsky."

Fields nodded, more focused than ever because when she was researching that case, there had been so many redactions in the records that they were worthless.

"You know there have always been rumors, but nothing substantial enough to actually start an investigation. But what happened with that poor girl, it didn't add up. So, we—"

"Who's we?" Steel interrupted.

"NSA. We started snooping around, off the record. We'd find a lead, and then it would just evaporate. Didn't make sense. They operate in complete anonymity, invisible, seemingly invincible, so far outside the law as to be inconceivable they could even exist."

"How?"

"I have my ideas, but honestly, I don't know. We're still, or let me clarify, *I'm* still in the middle of the investigation."

"You're on this by yourself?" Fields asked, astonished.

Todd nodded. "From the get-go. I decided I couldn't risk having anyone else involved."

"Me too!" Fields blurted out. "Me too. The only other person I've ever even talked to about this is with Steel."

Steel nodded.

"I knew I wasn't crazy."

"No, you're not," Todd assured her. "Would you mind running down your notes for me?"

"Absolutely," Fields answered immediately, giving Todd the full breakdown of what she'd discussed with Steel during their lunch in Newport.

"Impressive," Todd told her as she wrapped things up.

Steel chimed in, "I have to admit, given what's happened in the past twelve hours, it all seems a lot more feasible, even more serious, than it did when you initially ran it by me."

"It's as serious as it gets," Todd assured him. "Even with all the resources I have at my disposal, this is as far as I've gotten."

"What do you mean?"

"I'm just one of their pawns."

"You're head of fucking NSA. How can you just be a pawn?"

"Being head of NSA is what opened the door. It's what got me in initially, and it's taken all these years for me to even get to where I am now."

"So, these guys are careful?"

"Beyond. Beyond anything I've ever encountered. In the scheme of things, I'm no one. Like I said, a pawn, nothing more than an errand boy."

"How did you figure it out?"

"I'm not even close to having it figured out. But back when I started the investigation, after a few years, I uncovered a pattern, or at least what I thought were some possible patterns, events that just seemed too random to be random. The deeper I looked, the less I found. No links. Nothing connecting anything or anyone of interest I was looking into. As you both know all too well, in any investigation, it's finding a common denominator, anything that connects the dots."

"And?"

"And the only thing—and I mean the only thing—those leads I was tracking had in common was sex. They'd all been caught in some sort of sexual scandal."

Pulling Steel's shoulder around so she could see his face, Fields said, "I told you. I knew it!"

"Knew what?" Todd asked.

"I put together an endless list of politicians together, dating back a hundred years, who were all caught fucking around in one way or the other, basically ending their careers."

"Interesting," Todd said. "My money is on our lists being almost identical."

"No doubt," Fields said. "But I haven't been able to come up with anything that connects them other than they were all in politics."

"I hadn't either."

"So what did you do?" Steel asked.

"I concentrated on the only thing that they all did have in common, and that was the sex."

"Pretty much includes the entire world population," Steel chimed in. "Good luck with that one."

"No doubt," Todd said with a little grin, "but as it turns out, several persons of interest all enjoyed visiting a little place called The Spa."

"No shit?" Fields said, dumbfounded, furious at herself for not making the connection herself. "That's brilliant."

"Turns out, the Spas are all over the country."

"There are a dozen spas here in Newport alone," Steel rebutted. "They're fucking everywhere."

"You're absolutely right. In fact, in the US alone we have over twenty-one thousand licensed spas, but only a dozen elite palaces known as *The* Spa."

"So?"

"So, I joined."

"Just like that?"

"Yep. Anyone can just walk in the front door and sign up. Become a member and become one of the pampered few."

"That's too easy."

"Exactly. It's part of the reason I've concluded why they're so successful and part of the sixteen-billion-dollar annual spa business."

Steel was dumbfounded, shaking his head. "I've driven by that place a thousand times and never given it a second thought."

"Another reason for their success. They're hiding in plain sight, open doors to anyone and everyone with the means to pay for a spa day. But hiding deep within those walls, and walls around the world just like the ones in Fashion Island, flows a life blood that determines the course of world events."

"How? By setting presidents up with hookers?"

Todd shot Steel a cold stare.

"Sorry, man," Steel apologized. "I didn't mean it like that."

Todd never took his eyes off him, taking a deep breath before speaking. "In essence, Detective Steel, you're correct. Last night, why we're here right now, is proof positive these men exist."

"I'm trying. I really am, but I'm sorry. I'm still not buying it."

"Through whatever means necessary, the Elite obtain career-ending dirt on everyone from politicians to corporate CEOs. No one is off limits."

"And if there isn't any dirt?"

"They manufacture it."

"How?"

"By discretely offering men the one thing they simply can't refuse—beautiful young bodies, no complications, no strings."

"If what you're claiming is even partially true, and these men, these Elites, as you call them, conduct worldwide, undetectable covert operations involving individuals at the highest levels, then what the hell happened last night? That was a complete cluster fuck."

"No doubt," Todd admitted openly. "But it did confirm one thing."

"And what's that?" Fields questioned him.

"They didn't anticipate me throwing a wrench into their plans."

"Just so I'm getting this straight. You're the head of the NSA, and you're an undercover double agent acting totally on your own, investigating what you believe to be is an elite group of men who control the world?"

Todd grinned facetiously. "And there's a rogue element within the Elites."

"Rogue?"

"I've had a feeling about it ever since that kid came out of nowhere and won the election eight years ago."

"I thought you just said your guys were invincible."

"I thought so, but after some of the things that happened in Chicago leading up to that election, I started wondering who is really in control."

"And?"

"And time after time during the last eight years, events that transpired just didn't add up, things the Elites would never allow to happen. Last night confirmed it. The Elites have somehow been compromised. They're in a raging battle for control within their own organization against the group I'm calling the Chicago Elites."

"Versus just the regular Elites?" Fields asked sarcastically. "Not to mention, you're soon to be, if not already, now at the top of the FBI's most wanted list."

"Let's not forget the CIA and Homeland Security," Todd added with a smile. "I did kick the president of the United States in the nuts and run off with his girlfriend."

"Brilliant," Fields added.

"And you've put us right in the middle of this little power struggle?" Steel chimed in.

Todd closed his eyes. "Smack dab in the middle of the biggest jackpot I've ever seen."

"Great. Thanks for that," Steel added, seeing his career coming to an abrupt end. "So what are we going to do?"

"I'm not sure, but I have an idea that just might work—if we can stay alive long enough to make it happen."

***

"We have a hit on their phones," a young agent behind one of a hundred plus computer screens inside Langley's critical ops room yelled instantly as the bag of phones came online in Midway.

"Where?" the agent in charge asked, hurrying to the alerting agent's screen.

"Midway Island."

"Deploy now! Lock 'em down! No one leaves that island. You understand, no one."

"Yes, sir."

***

"One of their phones just came online," announced a far more controlled voice from behind another screen in another equally impressive control center far away from Washington.

"Location?"

"Midway. It just popped."

"Whose?"

"The FBI agent's, Fields."

"What about the others?"

"No."

"Active?"

"No, sir. It just came online."

"Okay. Let me know when there's any traffic on it."

"Roger."

About fifteen minutes later, "Sir, the other three just popped."

"Location?"

"Same. Midway Atoll."

"All three at the same time?"

"Yes, sir."

"It's not them."

***

By the time the cavalry arrived at Midway, there wasn't a trace of the Citation or the supply ship—only the sole bewildered airport maintenance man who didn't speak English holding a bag of cell phones he'd found in the restroom.

***

As the vile slowly warmed up in the pilot's pocket and Jewels' tracers thawed out, coming back online, their signals were immediately picked up by the Elites.

"We got her," came the excited announcement.

"Where?"

"Panama City."

"How many signals?"

"All three."

"Is she on the move?"

"Ahh, stand by. No, sir. She seems to be stationary."

"Exact location."

"Panama International. Terminal Two. Concorde level. Departures. Singapore Airlines. Gate G-Ninety-Nine, sir."

"When is that flight scheduled to leave?"

"Closing doors now, sir."

"Get a team on it just to be sure, but it's a decoy."

"Yes, sir."

Chapter 14

Todd pulled out one of the disposable cell phones they'd bought in Avalon. "Any chance of getting a signal back here?" he asked Steel.

"Not tucked in here. No way. Either need to get out a couple miles from under these cliffs or hike to the top of the ridge."

Surveying the single track, an almost vertical climb up the cliffs leading away from the cove to the top to the backside of the island, Todd's thoughts were interrupted by Steel. "Be a lot easier, if we just run the dinghy out a couple miles."

"Agreed."

***

A few minutes later, the two men were floating about two miles off the backside of Catalina Island in the dinghy.

***

"Sir, unsecured, incoming for you on your personal line."

Knowing that only a few individuals in the world had that number, the Elite knew it was Todd before he even answered.

"Go ahead."

"I have the girl, whom you cannot have. I have the DNA and her sworn testimony she was raped by the president last night, both of which are yours. You have the video; that's all you'll need to destroy him."

He was stalling for time, knowing they needed eighteen seconds to trace the call. "Without the girl, none of that will stand up in court."

"Fuck you," Todd said, hanging up.

"Goddammit!" screamed the Elite into the dead line, glancing at his tech team, knowing they hadn't had time to get any tangible data on Todd's location.

***

"Nice conversation," Steel said, nodding approval at Todd, liking him more and more. "Is that really any way to talk to your superiors?"

Todd smiled. "Just wanted to let him know we were still on his team."

"And nothing inspires team spirit better than a hearty fuck you."

"I'm insulted he even tried that bullshit. This thing's never going to court."

"So, what's next?"

"We wait twenty-four hours and see what happens on the news cycle."

"That's your big plan for salvation? Sit back and watch TV?"

"Pretty much."

"Okay then."

"I told them what they needed to hear. They know the DNA is theirs. They're no longer exposed. After the Lewinsky ordeal, they learned their lesson—Get proof positive on multiple levels before going after anyone associated with Chicago."

Steel nodded that he understood. "But if I was to guess, I'd say your Elites are more interested in shutting down the Chicago contingency than the presidency."

"I think you're right. That rogue splinter is Chicago-based."

"But isn't the former secretary of state part of that whole deal?"

"She is, but she's going to self-destruct. Even if she gets elected, I think that organization is starting to come unraveled."

"Why?"

"Because they lost control of the guy they put in the Oval Office."

"How so?"

"The fucker's a narcissist, actually believes he's God. It's just a matter of time."

"Where does that leave us?"

"Not sure, but once Chicago knows the Elites have both his DNA and the video, the heat will be off us, or at least the bullseye. They want us dead for sure, but killing us now will only complicate things."

"So, just like that we're scot free?"

"Maybe," Todd said. "Probably not. I don't know. I'm finished, that's a given. Jewel's life will never be the same, but if we can survive the next twenty-four hours, we might get out of this mess with our lives. And at this point, that'll be more than enough."

Todd sensed Steel's concerns and continued explaining.

"For whatever's it worth. I've worked with these men for over two decades. They keep things clean and simple. Last night, breaking protocol, I threw a wrench into their operation. That's the only reason things went sideways. That entire cluster fuck was one hundred percent on me."

Steel looked hard into Todd's eyes. "What exactly was your plan last night?"

"To keep her by my side all night. I knew if I did some heads would roll, but no one would have gotten hurt. I just wanted to protect her, keep her away from the president, keep her safe."

"And you decided to do all this when?"

"On our way up in the limo."

"Seriously?"

"Yes, sir," Todd paused. "I haven't been able to get her out of my mind since we met, and seeing her again, being next to her, I just knew. I couldn't let anything happen to her."

"Funny the shit we do for love," Steel said.

Todd agreed, nodding. "It is. I knew what the assignment was last night. I knew it was coming, but she didn't. It wasn't right, letting her get blindsided like that. Something snapped when I saw that giant grab her."

"She's a pro," Steel said.

"She is. But being set up like that, being betrayed by her own people . . . by me, without her having a clue what she was getting herself into. I wouldn't have been able to live with myself if I hadn't tried to stop it. I knew their plan. It was brilliant. It would have worked. But when it was actually coming down," he continued, shaking his head, "I couldn't let it happen. It was wrong. She hadn't signed up for anything like that. I just couldn't let it go down."

"Admirable," Steel said, shrugging his shoulder, knowing Todd had sacrificed his entire career. "But honestly, if it had been anyone else?"

"We wouldn't be sitting here together off some island bobbing around in a rubber boat."

That made Steel smile, knowing he would have done the same thing for Fields. Looking around at the island in the near distance, he added, "Lot worse places to be."

***

212

The White House and the Untouchables were in a complete panic. The president's decree to shoot on sight had been issued against his advisors begging him not to. And just as they knew would happen, they were being bombarded with questions from every agency head in the government. The White House's initial "need to know only" position hadn't even begun to hold back the tidal wave of outcries. Within minutes after the order was issued, the media was up in full force, swarming the White House as well.

***

"Goddamned vultures," the president cursed as every line into the White House lit up.

His prized press room, where he'd virtually been unquestioned, loved, practically worshiped since taking office was overflowing with reporters wanting answers as to why an executive order to kill a decorated and devoted American citizen, the head of the NSA no less, who had served his country with nothing but distinction for decades, had been issued. The situation had exponentially gone from bad to worse for the lame duck president. In all his years, he'd never faced anything close to the mess he was in now. Up until now, the Chicago Elite had been able to control, buffer, and spin every national and international incident away from him. The president, always taking full credit for any positive achievements while pointing blame at others for any failures, was now carving a huge swath of scorched earth in his wake.

***

"You just couldn't keep it in your pants could you, you fucking asshole!" The first lady hissed at her unfaithful husband. "I can't believe you've ruined everything for a piece of ass. You are a fucking moron. Fuck you a thousand times over. I'm taking the kids and going to Hawaii."

"You can't leave now."

"Watch me, asshole. We're done. I'm filing for divorce."

"You can't. Not now. I need you more now than ever."

Flipping him her middle finger, she stormed out of their bedroom, leaving the president alone with his ice packs and cantaloupe balls. They were so swollen he couldn't even stand up to address the press, who were demanding a personal appearance.

***

His advisors began jumping ship the second their commander in chief demanded the order be issued. In fact, the initial leaks had come from his inner circle, individuals scrambling to distance themselves as far and as fast as they could from him. The carefully crafted world of the current presidency, a world the Chicago Elite had spent years building, was crumbling. To say they were pissed could be considered the understatement of all time. Combine this with the fact his heir apparent was collapsing during public outings, unraveling their entire plans that took years of groundwork, manipulation, and billions of carefully spent dollars in order to meticulously weave their agenda into the very fabric of America's political, social and economic leaders, they couldn't let that happen.

***

The Elites had been in communication within their inner circle since the onset of the mission. When Todd pulled the girl from under the president, their initial reaction was shock, followed by pure disgust for having had their top field operative turn on them. But as events continued unfolding, all in their favor, sentiments were quickly changing.

"He may have done more for us last night than we'll ever know."

"It appears that could be a distinct possibility. But nonetheless, results don't dismiss the fact that he failed to follow orders. To me, there's no question; he's done."

"I agree. As an operative, he's finished, but let's hold off making any final decisions right now; he's earned that much from us."

"He has the DNA."

"It's ours whenever we want it."

"How can you be sure?"

"He offered it if we wanted it."

"In return for what?"

"For leaving the girl out of it. For whatever reason, he's protecting her."

"Understood."

"The way things are unfolding for the president, we may not need either one."

"Still, I want to bank it."

"Agreed."

"What about the girl?"

"Let's wait and see what happens."

***

"How did you and Todd meet?" Fields asked Jewels.

Glancing from Samantha to Agent Fields, Jewels rolled her eyes, deciding to tell the truth, knowing how silly her secret agent life was going to sound to a real FBI agent. "On assignment," she said.

"On assignment?" Fields asked.

"Yeah," Jewels said, nodding her head.

"So you and Todd work together?"

"Before last night, only once."

Fields nodded slowly, trying to fill in between the lines. "Interesting."

Samantha jumped in, "What about you and Steel?"

"On assignment," Fields answered with a little grin.

"Interesting," Jewels answered immediately, this being the first opportunity the two women had had to size one another up.

"Touché," Fields responded before deciding to open up. "The bureau's investigating some high-end escort services that led us to Newport."

A cold chill shot up Jewel's spine.

"Really," Samantha said, "do tell."

"I can't comment on an ongoing investigation."

"Oh, come on," Samantha begged. "Just between us girls. Off the record."

Afraid Fields was reading her like a book, Jewels chimed in, trying to sound as casual as possible, "Yeah, off the record."

Fields gave her a short intense look while deciding what she was going to tell them before speaking. "Appears there's a pretty buttoned-up service working the waterfront."

"Really," Samantha said, admitting, "I had no idea."

"Me neither," added Jewels.

"Not surprising," Fields said, still deciding if she should cut the conversation short. Given last night's events, she thought to herself, *Could these women be a part of it?*

"Off the record?" She confirmed one last time.

Both women nodded in agreement simultaneously.

"Okay. I can't go into specifics, but suffice it to say that it appears the willing gentlemen of Newport are being well taken care of."

"Not surprising," Samantha said, "given how financially influential the area is. No different than in any other major city."

"But why the FBI?" Jewels asked innocently. "Wouldn't something like that be left to local authorities?"

Fields nodded in agreement. "Yeah. Normally, the bureau wouldn't have anything to do with something like this."

"So what's up?"

"Honestly, I wish I knew," Fields told them, keeping her theories to herself for the time being.

"So, what do you have?" Samantha asked.

"Not much," Fields answered truthfully. "Nothing out of the ordinary, a madam discreetly running a handful of girls. As far as I could tell, nothing we needed to be involved with."

Jewels and Samantha nodded in agreement.

"After spending the day with Steel and his team last week and reporting back to my boss, we were pulled off the assignment . . . that was, until last night."

"What do you mean?"

"Come on," Fields asked pointedly. "You tell me."

"I don't know what you're talking about," Jewels said defensively.

"You're telling me last night was all just happenstance? Your date with Todd . . . the president?"

"Fuck you," Jewels snapped, fists clinched, stepping towards Fields. "Those assholes grabbed me, and that motherfucker raped me!"

Samantha immediately wedged herself between the two. Todd and Steel pulled up in time to catch Jewels' outburst.

"Whoa," both men yelled as they sprung out of the inflatable, each stepping in front of their respective fighters.

Todd put his arms around Jewels, looking inquisitively into her eyes.

"She accused me of being …" She broke down in tears before she could finish her sentence.

Todd, still holding Jewels securely, turned around, facing Fields and Steel.

"She had nothing to do with what happened last night. She didn't have a clue."

Fields and Steel remained silent.

"I set her up."

"What?" Jewels whispered in disbelief.

"I'm so sorry," Todd said, looking her in the eyes. "I'm so sorry."

Tears still filled Jewel's eyes. Her heart breaking, she slowly backed away from the man she'd fallen madly in love with— the man she was realizing she knew nothing about. Samantha stepped around Todd and held her best friend. Jewel's head involuntarily turned from side to side in denial.

"Jewels, please," begged Todd.

"No," she said flatly. "You don't get to say you're sorry. You set me up," she continued more to herself than Todd.

"Jewels."

"What kind of person does something like that?" Her heart shattering into fragments, Jewels slowly turned away from the man whom she thought she'd be spending the rest of her life with and walked out to the cockpit with Samantha.

Todd felt his soul leaving his body. He could hardly breathe, but he didn't care. After decades of being alone, he'd finally found a woman he admired and loved more than life itself, and in spite of doing everything he could, he'd failed. Nothing would ever change what he'd allowed to happen to her last night. She was right. No words would ever be able to erase the horror she'd experienced.

218

Chapter 15

Humphrey Bogart's classic line from "Casablanca" summed it up in one sentence, *"It doesn't take much to see that the problems of three little people don't amount to a hill of beans in this crazy world."*

Sitting quietly around the salon watching the end of one of the greatest love stories of all time, Jewels came to terms with herself. Throughout dinner, the conversation had been hushed, nothing more having been said about the night before. Exhaustion set in after almost thirty-six sleepless hours for the five lives onboard the *Vintage*, which was now resting contentedly at anchor, her hull gently rising and falling with a soothing swell that mimicked the sea's beating heart. The heavens showered down an endless canopy of diamonds, reflecting off the calm waters surrounding them in the little cove, their sixty-by-twenty-foot world of wood and fiberglass securely cradled in the wings of an angel. Even though she'd been deceived, Jewels knew she was still in love with Todd. Nothing could ever change what happened last night, but the more she thought things through, her feelings of anger and betrayal slowly dissolved.

Love has a way of taking on a life of its own. Despite how bad we want something, sometimes things unfold in ways we never imagine. We're all a part of the fabric that bonds us, weaves us together, she thought to herself, recognizing right then and there she didn't want to live without him. As Bogart and Claude Rains walked across that wet runway in Casablanca on the tv, Jewels reached out, taking Todd's hand, helping him up off the couch, gently kissing him as the last lines of the movie echoed in their ears . . . *Louis, I think this is the beginning of a beautiful friendship.*

She led him below and into one of the staterooms.

***

The dawn broke with a serene silence—not a wisp of wind, not a cloud being revealed behind the fading darkness surrendering slowly to the first rays of a new day.

"What do you think?" Jewels asked sleepily without opening her eyes.

Todd had been awake for a while, listening in the silence. "Umm, good morning, sunshine," he said, kissing her gently.

"Are we going to make it? Honestly," Jewels said, rolling into his arms, "if it all ends right now."

"One night and you're done with me?"

"Oh, *contraire*," she said, lightly kissing his face. "I'm never letting you go."

"I wouldn't let you if you tried."

Kissing deeply, they melted into one another again.

***

Waking up in excoriating pain, the president screamed, "Where the fuck are they?" demanding to be updated on the situation. "It's been over twenty-four hours and nothing. Not a word!"

"Sir."

"Don't sir me," he continued, hammering his chief. "I ordered that asshole killed. How the hell did he just vanish into thin air?"

"Sir."

"They left the party with the fucking FBI, for Christ's sake. Why the fuck didn't she shoot him? Where the hell is that agent anyway? Get her on the line."

His chief paused.

"Well?" the president snapped demandingly.

"She's missing, sir."

"What do you mean she's missing?"

"The department hasn't heard from her since last night. No sign of the vehicle."

"Why don't they just ping her? Ping the fucking car."

"No signal."

"I don't believe this shit."

"Sir, the situation has become more complicated than we initially thought."

"It's not complicated. Find the bastard that did this to me," the president snipped, glancing down at the ugly black-and-blue grapefruits that used to be his testicles, "and kill the motherfucker."

"Sir, we have no proof."

"What do you mean we don't have any proof? What about the fucking tapes?"

"The AIC killed the feed before the incident."

"He what?!"

"Killed the feed, sir. We have no footage."

This gave the president pause. "Are you positive?"

"Absolutely, sir, no footage of the attack."

"So there is some footage?'

"Yes, sir. Everything leading up to . . ." His chief of staff hesitated, looking for the right words. "Up until you and the young lady became . . . engaged."

"Shit," the president said, hoping for a moment that if there wasn't any footage he might have an out with his handlers.

"Sir, it's blowing up. You need to rescind that order."

The president screamed, "That motherfucker attacked me. He dies. Period."

***

Plant a bomb at the finish line of the Boston marathon where bloody carnage of innocents is replayed over and over for the world to see, no one thinks twice about shutting down an entire city to find the cowards that did it. Doesn't matter who you are. When something like that happens, Americans band together as a family, as one. We fight like brothers and sisters amongst ourselves, but when strangers attack, we have no mercy. It's in our DNA. It's part of what makes us who we are, what makes us a great country.

In Todd's case, an order by the commander in chief to kill an American citizen on sight, on American soil, without any explosions, bombings, evidence of wrongdoing or even misconduct, was simply too much. But the President had come to believe he was destined to change this country forever, that he was the chosen one. And after successfully driving another Alinsky stake into the hearts of the nation on December 11, 2016, with another executive order revoking the federal government's recognition of, and banning of, the Pledge of Allegiance from public schools, he believed nothing could stop him now, and wasting one little government servant wasn't even an issue.

Fortunately for Todd and his little band of misfits, the wheels of justice, by design, turn very slowly. Even though an executive order had been decreed from the White House, the order was being viciously contested within the halls of government. Talk about throwing a monkey wrench into the system. Internal hell was breaking loose within every department, agency, and branch of the military. Even though an order may ultimately prove in a court of law to be unconstitutional, disregarding an order from the commander in chief is, by definition, a treasonable offense. A line had been crossed. There was no middle ground. Either you stood blindly behind the president or you didn't, and that ship was sinking fast. Even his Untouchables were running for lifeboats. Legal analysts were going nuts. Every news media and digital service was consumed by the order. Dissension began running rampant, from department heads to rank and field officers. This was so wrong.

***

None of which was going unnoticed by the Chicago Elite as they discussed the situation on their encrypted lines.

"He's lost it."

"We have to get a handle on this now before he blows the entire election."

"It might be too late already."

"We isolate her. Pull her away from it all. She can't have anything to do with him from here on out."

"Keep her on point and we should be alright."

"But he's done. Shut him down."

"Agreed."

***

Equally as fortunate for Todd and the gang was the fact the Chicago Elite's decisions were executed with lightning speed and efficiency. Within minutes after making their decision, every contact they'd spent a decade establishing within the government, law enforcement, and the military had been given the word: "Disregard the president's order. He's finished." The system at work. Order restored.

***

After the movie, Steel and Fields had headed topside. "It's beautiful," Fields said as they stretched out on the queen-sized pad behind the wheelhouse, looking out across the sparkling water surrounding them.

"It is," Steel agreed, nodding. "About as good as it gets," he added, "at least for me."

"I can see why you love this boat so much. I honestly had no idea."

"What do you mean?"

"I've never spent a night on a boat before. This is a first for me."

Steel took her hand. "You know, you've ruined it for me."

"Ruined what."

"This." He said gesturing out around them. "The magic."

"I don't understand."

"It's never going to be the same for me again."

"Now you're starting to piss me off. Just say what you mean."

"Having you here, it'll never be the same without you."

Those simple words melted her heart. Without hesitation, she turned towards him, pulling his lips to hers.

***

Having been the only one onboard to have gotten a full night's sleep, Samantha started her morning off in the galley. The wonderful, intoxicating aroma of bacon frying in the salt air was enough to wake everyone onboard. As the couples came into the salon, Samantha greeted them with a delicious mug of fresh-brewed coffee. Sliced fruit was on the table. She was taking egg orders as she pulled a batch of steaming hot buttermilk biscuits from the oven.

"Just like camping," she said cheerfully, "only better."

"Delicious," Jewels said, sipping her coffee. "Let me help you."

"Thanks, I've got it," Sam said. "Not enough room in here for two anyway."

"Ture," Jewels answered.

"By design," Steel chimed in. "On a boat this size, any galley that can handle more than one cook at a time was laid out wrong."

Conversation continued causally throughout breakfast, but as everyone leaned back after eating, the stark circumstances of their situation came to the forefront.

"Any ideas?" Steel asked Todd.

"Wish we could catch the morning cycle," Todd answered. "It would help if we knew what the rest of the world was watching."

"We could run out in the dinghy again, and I could check in," Steel offered. "I haven't been compromised, so we should be okay."

Suddenly worried, Todd asked, "You didn't bring your cell with you, did you?"

Steel shot Todd a look that said it all. "I may be slow, but I'm not stupid. Left it in my truck at the marina."

"Sorry," Todd said apologizing immediately. "Good idea, let's run out there."

"I want to go," Jewels said.

"Me too."

"You're not leaving me behind," Fields said. "Can we all fit?"

"Easily, no problem," Steel told her with a little kiss on the cheek.

Fifteen minutes later, they were all in the dinghy on their way out of the protected cove, heading offshore just far enough to catch a signal off the island's southernmost tower. A school of dolphin greeted them on their way out, coming up close enough off their bow to catch a little bit of spray from exhales.

"This is beyond," Fields said excitedly. "So cool."

"They're such beautiful creatures."

"Oh my God!" screamed Samantha. "Look! A baby and her mom."

Sure enough, a baby dolphin surrounded by several adults swam right up to and under their bow.

***

After his first couple years in office, the president had gotten over his fear of the red phone ever ringing, learning that if the situation ever did arise, the events leading up to causing it to ring would have been on the radar far in advance. What he thought he'd gotten over and hadn't even thought about since sweeping his reelection was fear of his *other* red phone ringing. When it did, he about crapped himself. There was only one person in the world that had access to that number, his handler.

"This is the president."

"Think I don't know who'd answer this phone." It wasn't a question.

"I can explain—" said the president.

"Shut the fuck up!"

"But—"

In a cold, controlled voice that left absolutely no doubt about meaning every word, the caller interrupted, "I said shut up, or your next breath will be your last."

Frantically spinning around, the president looked for the threat. Not seeing anything out of the ordinary, he knew if the threat had been made, it was real. Starting to speak, he caught himself. No one had spoken to him like that in years, except his wife . . . *the ungrateful bitch*. He'd surrounded himself with yes men, and his Untouchables made damn sure anyone in his company displayed only the highest respect. He'd come to think of himself as royalty, when in reality he'd become a spoiled, pampered brat, the world at his feet.

"You're a fucking moron," said his handler, hoping to entice him to speak so he could give the nod to have him killed on the spot and be done with him.

Silence.

After a prolonged pause. "Good decision, *Mr. President*. You just saved your own life—or at least bought yourself a little more time."

Silence.

"Nice to see you can still follow a simple instruction."

The president was seething inside but controlled himself. Silence.

"The others said you were too young, too full of yourself to ever really make a difference," he continued, still baiting him.

Silence.

"I fought for you. I was wrong. They were right." He was still hoping again for a reaction.

Silence.

Bitterly disappointed thinking about the enormous amounts they'd spent making him president, and most recently the groundwork they'd laid to move him onto the ticket as vice president had been wasted, he continued, "Retract that ridiculous kill order on Windham and get the fuck out of the way."

Silence.

Spineless piece of shit. "You're finished."
The line went dead.

***

A few hours later, the announcement from July 23, 2016: (CNN) Democratic presidential candidate chooses Virginia senator to be her running mate, turning to a steady and seasoned hand in government to fill out the . . .

***

Putting the burner on speaker, Steel dialed headquarters, knowing none of his team would pick up an unidentified number if he'd called any of their personal cells directly.

"Newport Beach Police Department, how may I direct your call?"

"Steel here. Are Laughlin or Hale around?"

"Hey, Detective. How are you doing?" the receptionist asked casually.

"Fine, what's up?"

"Nothing. Same ol' same ol'.'"

"Really?" Steel asked.

"Yeah, pretty much back to normal after that cluster yesterday."

Playing dumb, mining for information, Steel asked, "What happened?"

"You weren't here?" the receptionist asked.

"No. I was off."

"Oh my God," she said. "It was insane."

"Everyone alright?"

"Oh yeah, nothing like that."

"Then what was it?"

"The Feds. They swept in here first thing in the morning, causing all sorts of problems."

"What did they want?"

"At first, no one had a clue. They locked down the place."

"You're kidding me."

"Not even. Machine guns out and all. Full SWAT mode. It was totally intense."

"I can only imagine."

"Yeah, everyone standing around staring at one another. You could have cut the tension with a knife. Way too many guns and too much testosterone in a small space, as far as I was concerned."

"What did you do?"

"Nothing. I froze. Didn't move."

"Then what?"

"They walked into the chief's office like they owned the place. I swear if his office hadn't had glass walls so the men could all see what was happening, it could have gone bad really fast. They talked to the chief for a couple minutes, and when they came out, he told us everything was okay."

"That's it?"

"Hardly. Somehow—and don't ask me how, because the chief is still screaming for details—the Feds said there were some tests run from our lab that came back positive for the president's DNA."

"No way."

"I swear to God. Can you believe that? The president. They wanted his DNA."

"And?"

"And nobody knew shit. Nada."

"So, what happened?"

"Chief demanded if anybody knew anything about it to step forward, but nobody did. I think that embarrassed him—you know, not knowing what's going on in his own department. He was pissed."

"I can only imagine. So, what did the Feds do?"

"They said it was of highest national security and told the chief—they didn't ask, they told him—they were going to search the place."

"He didn't fight them, but I could tell he was fuming. He agreed so long as his officers and staff could get back to work."

"They posted guards at all the doors and actually frisked everyone going out."

"Bet that went over well."

"Not too bad actually, but then they wouldn't let anyone into the building. I mean no one—not even our guys."

"That's bullshit."

"Yeah, no one was very happy, but it was obvious they were dead serious on finding that DNA."

"Did they find it?"

"Hell no. Nobody knew shit. After a few hours, it became apparent they'd gotten some bad intel."

"That sounds insane. Glad I missed it."

"Yeah, you are."

"So, what finally happened?"

"They were still searching the place when all of a sudden their boss announced, 'We're done. Let's go.'"

"Just like that?"

"Just like that. Right in the middle of the search, they just dropped everything they were doing and left. Gone as quickly as they came in."

"No shit?"

"That's what everyone thought. So weird. Like trained dogs called off the hunt. This morning, when I came in, everything was back to normal. Hang on, the board is lighting up. I'll transfer your call."

"Okay, thanks."

"Detective Hale."

"It's Steel."

"Hey, boss. What's up?"

"Just checking in."

"You missed all the fun yesterday."

"I heard."

"Insane. It was fucking nuts. Thank God cooler heads prevailed. It could have gone south real quick."

"Nobody likes having MP-Fives pointed at them."

"Damn straight."

"Everyone okay?"

"Roger, boss. But it was touch and go there for a few minutes."

"I can't even imagine."

"But it's all good now."

"Thanks. Anything else going on?" Steel asked, still digging for more info.

"No. Nothing unusual. Why are you calling in through the main line?" the young detective asked casually.

"Left my damn cell in the truck."

"Dumbass," Hale said, poking fun. "That's not like you."

"I know. Boneheaded move."

"When you back?"

"Tomorrow or next day."

"Cool. You over at the island?"

"Yep."

"Okay. Enjoy yourself."

"Always do over here. Thanks," Steel said, hanging up.

"That's interesting," Todd said.

"Have to agree," Steel confirmed, "other than a little FBI raid on our headquarters, sounds like business as usual."

"Your guy would have said something," Fields inquired, "had the story broken nationally, don't you think?"

"Absolutely."

"Everyone's playing it close to the vest," Todd said.

"Leaving us where?"

"Not sure," Todd answered.

"So, we're going to be okay?" Jewels asked hopefully.

Shaking his head slowly, Todd said, "Honestly, I don't know. It's uncharted waters. The fact the Feds pulled out without completing their search tells me they got orders from above."

"No other reason they would have left," Fields confirmed.

"So where would those orders have to come from?" Todd asked Fields.

"From the highest level."

"Meaning a direct order from the White House."

"Yep."

"They called off the dogs. That doesn't make any sense," Todd said out loud. "Why?"

"Maybe because no one knows exactly what happened at that party," Fields asked.

"They know. It's all on tape."

"What if they decided there's no upside to making a federal case out of it?"

"The president wouldn't let something like this slide," Steel interjected. "Way too big an ego."

"Unless . . ." Todd said, thinking out loud. "Unless the Chicago Elite made the decision for him."

"They have that kind of control?"

"Absolutely," Todd confirmed. "He was their chosen one. Without them, he'd still be passing out flyers as a community advocate."

"So what does that mean? They're done with him?"

Todd thought about it. "That makes sense. Keep him quiet, keep the noise down to protect his apparent heir. They don't need a scandal breaking right now. They practically have the election locked up."

"I wouldn't be so sure," Steel said.

"But it would be hard to protect her from the fallout if a scandal like this broke so close to the election."

"Which brings us to the question, what are," Todd said, shaking his head for not having a better term, "what are *my* Elite going to do."

"Time for another call?" Steel asked.

***

"Once again," Todd said when his call was answered, "I have the girl. You can't have her. She's off limits and officially retired, as am I. We're both out of the game. Period. No questions asked. No harm. No foul."

"In exchange for what?"

"The president's DNA."

Pause.

"When?"

"I'll have it delivered tomorrow."

Long pause.

"Deal." The line went dead.

***

"That's it?" Jewels asked Todd.

Todd smiled at her. "Yep. It's over."

"Just like that?"

"Yep. They got what they wanted."

"I can't believe it," Jewels said, throwing her arms around him. "I won't have to testify or anything?" she asked innocently.

"No," he said, knowing it would have never come to that anyway. "You're safe and clear of this entire mess."

"Thank you, thank you, thank you," she said, showering him with kisses.

***

Heading back to the boat, Todd asked Steel, "Mind doing us a little favor?"

Steel looked suspiciously at Todd. "Depends."

"When you get back to the office, ask your chief to deliver this little package to The Spa for me."

"You've got to be kidding me? Why the chief."

"Let's just say he has a long and personal relationship with the folks over there."

Steel slowly shook his head. "I'm getting too old for this shit." He looked Fields in the eye, asking, "How about you?"

Fields nodded. "Me too, but . . ." She paused, looking around the little cove as they approached the boat. "But I could get used to this."

"Okay then," Steel said, putting his arm around her, nodding at Todd. "I'd be glad to do it. I'll ask him to make the delivery as soon as we get back—when I tell him I'm retiring."

***

Pulling anchor, they had the boat underway in no time, rounding the East End, heading toward Newport.

"I've been thinking," Todd said, sitting alone with Jewels on the bow in the warm morning sun. "A friend of mine had to leave his plane at a resort on a remote little island down south. I kind of owe him. What do you say we head down, spend a little time there, and when we're ready, fly his plane home for him?"

"You're a pilot as well?"

"You're going to love seeing the Panama Canal; it's amazing."

***

Meanwhile in the salon . . .

Samantha was frantically writing notes. She had the storyline for her next script.

Review Requested:

We'd like to know if you enjoyed the book.
Please consider leaving a review on the platform
from which you purchased the book.

CPSIA information can be obtained
at www.ICGtesting.com
Printed in the USA
BVHW032348130621
609504BV00005B/24/J

9 781682 354001